A Lady & Her Sire

The Aftermath

Part 4

A Novel By

Charmanie Saquea

Text **ROYALTY** to 42828 to

join our mailing list!

To submit a manuscript for our review, email us at

submissions@royaltypublishinghouse.com

Text RPHCHRISTIAN to 22828 for our CHRISTIAN ROMANCE novels!

Text RPHROMANCE to 22828 for our INTERRACIAL ROMANCE novels!

Acknowledgements

First I would like to thank God for blessing me with the talent of being an author. Here I am on book number 31, none of this would have been possible without him.

To my mommy, Sheree, who has been by my side since day one, you told me I could be anything I wanted to be if I put my mind to it. You have always been my backbone and I would not have made it this far without you. Also my Grammy, you've been there every step of the way and I can't thank you two enough.

A HUGEEE thank you and shout out to Porscha and everyone at Royalty, you all are awesome! The love and support is miraculous.

I definitely have to give a big shout out to my pen sisters and GANG; Treasure & Jah. You two will never know how hard you push me to do better with each book that I drop. I appreciate all the help, feedback and even the yelling because it helped me out a lot. No matter how many times I wanted to give up, you never allowed me to. I love you lots! Let's continue to stack chips and take trips

I definitely can't forget to thank all the loyal readers who have been riding with me since Official Girl. You guys have been my motivation to keep going and busting my pen. All the inboxes, comments, and wall post have never gone unnoticed and I appreciate them and you more than you will ever know.

Last but never least, my Angels in heaven, Cora (Mom), Romney (Riggz) and Marisa, Uncle Tyrone (Big Shep), and Dad. I pray that you continue to watch over me. I can't forget my cousin, Tyrein, keep your head up baby, 2034 will be here before you know it.

A Lady & Her Sire 4

Charmanie Saquea

Previously…

Sire

If it was one thing I hated, it was having my fate in another muthafucka's hands. I already knew what the outcome was going to be, so there was no need for us even going through all this bullshit. In this country, ain't no such thing as innocent until proven guilty for a black man. If you're not pale as fuck, you're already guilty in the eyes of the fucking law. It don't matter if you committed the crime or not. Just being black is a crime on its own.

"Let's go, Lewis," one of the deputies said, as he came in with my shackles.

I slowly stood up and let him do his thing. After he was finished putting my slave shackles on me, he grabbed me by my arm to lead me to the courtroom. I gave this Jethro looking muthafucka a look that let him know he better release some of that hold he had on me, before I shattered his fucking bones. I'm guessing he got the message because his goofy looking ass turned beet red, as he loosened his grip.

When we walked into the courtroom, my eyes automatically went to my family. Of course, my boys were there with my moms and pops, but I was zoomed in on her. Lady sat there next to my mom, trying to look strong, but I knew her better than that. Her eyes were puffy and her nose was red. She didn't have allergies, so I knew she had been crying. That alone had me feeling fucked up already. Lady was not the type to cry too much, and she hated showing her emotions. Before I sat down, she mouthed the words 'I love you' to me and I mouthed right back.

This was it for me, this was the moment of truth. After what seemed like a long ass trial of nothing but bullshit, today was my judgment day. The DA had no problems painting the picture of me being a monster, but he had no proof to support that shit. If he really knew who he was fucking with, he would've been cautious as to what he let fly out of his fucking mouth. It would be nothing for me to have his ass killed as he was walking down the courthouse stairs.

I knew this case was about to be a bunch of bullshit when they brought in Lexus's distant ass sister that she didn't even fuck with, because she swore her sister wanted me. That bitch got on the stand doing all this fake ass crying and lying, talking about how I used to threaten her, and Lexus told her she was scared that I was going to do something to her. I knew the jury took that shit and ran with it because they were mostly women anyway. Since that bitch wanted to fuck with me, I gave Monty the go ahead to get rid of her ass. That bitch took my freedom as a joke, so I took her fucking life as a joke. Since she was faking like she missed her sister so much, I sent her ass to be with her.

Everything that they were saying was going right over my head. I had basically tuned everything out, because my mind wouldn't allow me to focus on what they were saying.

"Has the jury reached a verdict?" the judge asked.

I finally tuned everything back in when I heard that one. This was what everything boiled down to.

"Yes, your honor," she said. "On one count of second degree murder, the jury finds the defendant…guilty."

"What?" I heard Lady yell out behind me. "No, no, no!" she cried out.

I couldn't even turn around to look at her. I just stood there, stagnant and emotionless as the words replayed over in my head. *Guilty*. I had done a lot of fucked up shit in my lifetime, but I never thought that it would come back to bite me in the ass like this. I was actually going to spend the rest of my life behind bars for some shit that I really had no parts in. If I never believed karma was a bitch before, I damn sure believed the shit now.

"I'm so sorry, Sire. I really can't believe this shit right now. Don't worry though, I'll do everything we have to do to appeal this shit and get you home," Tracy said.

I couldn't even answer her because I was so fucked up. I had kids that I needed to get home to. I didn't have my sorry ass sperm donor in my life and didn't have a positive male role model until I went to live with Mama Nisa. I didn't want my kids growing up like me. I wanted them to be better than me, better than I ever was.

Then there was Lady. I couldn't leave her out here to take care of three kids on her own. She was going to need me, but yet, I was possibly spending the rest of my life behind bars. Would she stay down for me? Or would she fold and leave me while I'm at my lowest? Would she stay true to her words that she spoke to me while we were in Fiji? Shit, only time would be able to tell. I guess I just had to wait and see how this shit played out. I would be back though, and when I bounced back I was going to be better than ever. You can never keep a real nigga down for too long.

One – Sire

Two years later…

"Ninety-eight, ninety-nine, one-hundred," I counted, as I finished doing my daily set of push-ups.

Niggas wasn't lying when they said it wasn't shit to do in this bitch but work out. Since the first day they locked me up in this fucking cage, this was all I had been doing to help me keep my mind right and relieve some stress. It had been damn near three years since I slid into something tight, wet, and gushy, and I was beyond frustrated and backed up.

"Lewis!" one of the bitch ass guards yelled as he came to my cell. "Wrap this shit up, you got a visit."

I took my time getting up from the floor and used my shirt to wipe the sweat from my brow. One of my biggest struggles with being locked up was the fact that I had someone telling me what to do all the damn time. I was used to being the nigga that was calling all the shots and giving the orders, not answering to them. Of course, I was labeled as one of the most hardheaded and most defiant inmates in this bitch, but I really didn't give a fuck. I did shit on my own time and being locked up wasn't going to change that shit.

After getting myself together and freshening up, I was led out to the visiting room. A small smile spread across my face when I saw my little nappy headed ass brother sitting there with my mom. I was happy as fuck to see that Ry had finally convinced her to come see me. She said the sight of her son being locked up and not being able to bring me home with her was just too much for her to handle, so she wouldn't come see me. I understood where she was coming from and never held it against her, because I didn't want her to see me like this anyway. Now that I was seeing her, I couldn't be more happier.

"Ohh, my baby," she pouted, as she jumped up to hug me.

"Lewis! No touching!" another bitch ass guard yelled.

"Shut the fuck up and chill out," I spat in his direction.

"Kasire, don't. It's okay," my mom said as she sat down. "I don't want you getting into any trouble."

"I'm not gonna get in trouble, Ma. They want to put on a little act like they're in authority because it's a lot of people around, but they know who really running this bitch," I said, as I sat at the table with her and my brother.

"Same ol Kasire." She shook her head with a smile.

"You know how that go," I smiled with her. "What's up, little nigga? How's life treating you?" I asked Ry.

"Me? I'm good, what about you, though?" Ry questioned.

"I could complain but I'm not," I shrugged.

No lie, I was really fucked up about this shit. I still couldn't understand how the fuck I was found guilty for some shit that I never did. For this shit, I might as well should have gone ahead and killed the trifling bitch when I found out about her fucking Anton's bitch ass. If I could bring that nigga, Drill, back from the dead and kill his ass again for having me serve his sentence for him, since he was the one who actually killed Lexus, then I would.

"The rest of the goon squad sends their love. Toine said keep yo' head up," Ry said.

I didn't respond, but I nodded my head.

"How's everybody else doing, though?" I asked.

"Nigga, you should see your fucking kids. KJ and Kasim are us all over again. They be walking around terrorizing and fucking up shit, just like we used to. That terrible twos shit is real," Ry chuckled.

"Kasmira, though, she's a little diva," my mom chimed in. "She's a little Lady in the making, but she has an attitude out of this world."

I smiled as I thought about my daughter walking around with an attitude like her mama. I shook my head because I could only imagine the hell she was giving Lady. Since I had been locked up, I hadn't seen them or Lady. She tried to keep true to her word and hold me down, but I wasn't having it. I knew there was no chance of me getting out of this bitch anytime soon, so I cut her off and told her to just go ahead and live her life.

I let her know that if she did ever find someone new that he better treat her and my kids right, or I was going to send one of my niggas to put a fucking bullet in his head. It was one of the hardest things for me to do because I really loved her ass, but I refused to have her put her life on pause and wait for me, when we both knew damn well I wasn't leaving here, ever. I had already fucked up her life enough, so I wasn't going to do that to her.

"And Lady?" I asked, as I rubbed the back of my neck.

I had to mentally prepare myself for whatever I was about to hear. Even though I said I wanted her to move on, I don't think I was actually ready to hear that she had.

My mom and Ry exchanged looks and my mom shifted in her seat a little. I didn't know what that shit was about, but I knew I didn't like it.

"Sis is good. She holding shit down, taking care of the kids, finally went back to school and finished, got her own little business going on," Ry informed me.

I nodded my head in approval that Lady was actually doing something with her life. When we first got together and shit started getting hectic for us, she had dropped out of school, and it seemed as if she was never going to go back. I was happy and impressed by the fact that she was able to find time to go back between raising three kids. Even though my parents and brother helped out a lot, I knew it still couldn't have been easy for her. I hated that I had to leave her to raise three of my kids, one not even being hers, but there wasn't anyone else I trusted, besides my mom, to raise KJ, and I knew that she could handle it. She was built Ford tough.

"So what was up with that little look you and Ma just did? What, she got a new nigga or something?" I asked. That question had been burning in the back of my mind for the past year.

"Oh no, that's not hardly it. I highly doubt Lady is going to have a new man anytime soon. She has too much on her plate right now, and not to mention that she's still stuck on and in love with you," my mom let me know.

I fought hard to contain the smile that was threatening to spread across my face when my mom said that. I wasn't going to lie, every night I went to bed and woke up with Lady on my mind.

No matter how much I tried to push her out of my mind, it just wouldn't work. That damn girl had a hold on my heart that I didn't even know was possible.

For the rest of the visit, my mom and Ry spent time catching me up on everything that had been going on with the family. I was proud of how my brother and boys had been holding shit down in my absence. This wasn't the ideal situation for either of us, but it was what we had to deal with, no matter how fucked up it was.

Charmanie Saquea

Two – Lala

I stood over the stove cooking breakfast, when I felt a pair of strong arms wrap around my body, before a face was buried in my neck, placing soft kisses. I let out a small giggle before I turned around in his arms, kissing his juicy lips.

"Did you sleep good?" I asked.

"Hell yea! I wonder why." He smiled mischievously before slapping me on my ass.

I smiled bashfully before returning to cooking, while he took a seat at the table to watch me. After the whole situation with Toine went down two years ago, I never thought I would be able to find love again. I was so hurt and heartbroken with the way things went down between us, but God had sent me an angel from above.

Even though Darius and I have only been together for a little over a year, I was the happiest I had ever been in a while. He came into my life right on time. He was good to me and not to mention, he treated my kids like his own. That was what I loved most about him. At first I was a little apprehensive to start dating again, especially since I'd just had a baby and went through a horrible breakup.

Darius was very understanding of my situation though, and we started off just friends. What began so innocently, suddenly started to develop into something more. Before I knew it and could help myself, I had started to develop some very deep feelings for him and eventually came the love.

Of course, Antoine wasn't too happy to know that there was a new man in my life and it took him a while to come around to the idea. When he realized that there really wasn't an 'us' anymore, he finally accepted the idea that I had someone new.

"You gotta work today?" Darius asked me.

"Yea, I get off early today though," I let him know.

Just then, I heard the sounds of little pitter patter right before my little jovial Antoinette ran into the kitchen with AJ not too far behind her.

"Mommy, Mommy!" she yelled as she came running towards me.

I placed the spatula on the counter and swooped her up in my arms, placing kisses all over her little face. Antoinette let out a hearty laugh that caused her little funny colored eyes that she had inherited from her dad, to glisten. She may have looked like Toine, but her personality was all me.

"Good morning, baby girl," I said before placing her in her

seat. "Y'all sleep good?" I asked my kids.

"Yup."

"No."

They both answered at the same time. I couldn't help but to laugh at the scowl that was on AJ's face.

"She kept kicking me in my back and hogging all the cover," AJ said with an evident attitude.

Antoinette loved her brother so much that she often times refused to sleep in her own bed because she wanted to sleep with him. AJ loved her as well, but he hated sleeping with her because Antoinette was a wild sleeper. Often times I would go into her room in the middle of the night to check on her, and half of her body would be in the bed while the other half was on the floor.

"Well you—"

KNOCK, KNOCK, KNOCK!

My sentence was cut short by the sound of somebody knocking at my front door. I checked the time and saw that it was only nine in the morning, and nobody told me that they were coming over. With a confused face, I walked out of the kitchen to go see who was at my door.

"Toine, what are you doing here?" I asked, as I stood in the doorway with my arms folded.

Things between us for the most part were cordial. During the first year of our breakup, we remained close and were actually on a friend level, until Darius came in the picture, and that's when things between us started to change. Toine started acting funny, being distant and started having attitude problems all of a sudden. No matter how much he tried to say he was cool with me having a boyfriend, I knew deep down inside that he was feeling some type of way. It always showed through his actions, but I chose to ignore it.

"I came to get my kids," he said like that was a dumb question.

"Get them for what?" I questioned.

"I need a reason to get my own kids now?"

"No, but it would have been nice if you would've called to let me know you were coming or something," I let him know.

"I did, and you didn't answer the damn phone. Fuck you tripping for?" he asked as he walked up on me.

We stood there staring at each other as he glared down at me with those eyes I used to love so much. I don't know who he thought he was intimidating, but I was unmoved by him. Our little

24

stare battle could've went on for forever, but Darius's voice cut it short.

"What up?" he spoke to Toine.

Toine let out a little grunt that only I could hear. I squinted my eyes at him for being childish, but he ignored me. He pushed past me and made his way into the house, not bothering to speak back to Darius.

"They're not even dressed," I called after him.

"Don't nobody give a fuck but you," he said without turning around.

I looked over at Darius and he just shrugged his shoulders. Smacking my lips, I followed behind my worrisome baby daddy, as he made his way to the kids.

"Daddy!" Antoinette yelled with excitement while clapping her hands.

"Daddy's baby! What's good?" Toine asked, as he took her out of her seat, throwing her in the air.

Antoinette let out a squeal as she came back down, before wrapping her little arms around Toine's neck. I just stood back with a small smile on my face. One thing I could never take from Toine was the fact that he is a good ass father. No matter what we go through or what the status of our relationship is, he made sure to stay active in my kids' life. His other kids as well.

"Baby, I'm about to head out," Darius informed me. "I'll see you later. Maybe we can do lunch or something."

"Okay, I love you," I said as I fixed his collar.

"I love you too, girl," he said before placing a kiss on my lips.

The whole time, I could feel Toine burning a hole in the side of my face, but I paid him no mind. After Darius was gone, I went to fix me a plate of food.

"You eating?" I asked Toine with my back towards him.

"Nope, we about to get gone," he said in a sharp tone. "Junior, go get your shoes on and find your sister's for me."

"I get them, Daddy!" Antoinette yelled before jumping off his lap to follow behind her brother.

At just two years old, she was very independent. She always wanted to do things for herself and hated for somebody to do anything for her. I guess that was another trait you can say she got from me.

After fixing my plate, I sat at the table across from Toine and popped a piece of bacon in my mouth, as he continued to stare at me.

"So you love him?" he finally asked. "Shit that deep?"

"Toine—"

"Just answer the damn question, Alani," he cut me off.

"Yea, I do," I finally answered, looking him dead in the eyes.

Suddenly, the air in the room got thick and his light colored eyes started to get dark. I just shook my head because I knew that question was a setup, but yet, I fell for it anyways.

"Okay, Daddy! Ready!" Antoinette yelled as she came back into the room.

If things weren't so awkward at the moment, I would have laughed at the fact that she had her shoes on the wrong feet.

"I tried to put her shoes on for her, but she wouldn't let me," AJ announced.

"It's cool, let's go," Toine said, still glaring at me.

As AJ led the way out of the kitchen, I got up to put my plate away. I had suddenly lost my appetite. Before I could take another step, I was grabbed by my wrist and spun around. Toine was so close to me that I could smell the Listerine on his breath.

"Toine—"

"That nigga ain't gon' ever love you like I do," he cut me off. "Remember that shit while you up in this bitch playing house."

With that said, he turned around and made his exit. I stood there stuck, just letting his words marinate in my mind. A part of me still loved Toine and probably always would. He was my first everything and gave me two beautiful kids. The other part of me knew that nothing between us would probably ever be the same. We weren't teenagers anymore, and I just couldn't sit around and wait on him for forever.

A Lady & Her Sire 4

Three – Lady

Just landed...

I read over the text message once again as I stood in the pick-up section of the airport. Just as I was about to put my phone up, it buzzed with an incoming text message from my mom. I clicked on it and smiled when a picture of my kids popped up, as they smiled from ear-to-ear. Two years ago, the best thing I ever did was become a mother. I loved all three of my blessings, KJ included, because even though he wasn't my son by birth, he was still mine.

I will never forget the day that Lexus's mom tried to take him from me. It seemed as if she couldn't wait until Sire got locked up to pull some bullshit. Before Sire even got locked up, this lady was nowhere to be found or nowhere in the picture, but the moment she heard he was gone for a lengthy time, she came claiming that I wasn't KJ's birth mother, and she wanted her grandson. The saddest thing about it was that there was really nothing I could do because I wasn't KJ's mother.

My heart hurt so bad when they came and took KJ from my house that I swear I cried for three days straight. I had grown so attached to that little boy and loved him just as much as I loved the twins. Three days after he was removed from my home, Ry showed up at my front door with KJ and some papers his grandmother signed. I didn't understand what the hell was going on, but it wasn't hard for me to put two and two together on if Ryan was involved. Next thing I knew, I received some papers in the mail from Sire saying that I had his permission to adopt KJ.

It was a long and tedious process; they took me through a lot of loops, but it was worth it in the end. Now Kasire Armone Lewis Jr. was legally my son.

"Lady," I heard from behind me, accompanied by a tap on my shoulder.

"Hey, Lace," I smiled as I hugged my brother.

Initially, with everything that was going on with Sire and his case, I had put the search for my long lost brother on hold. I had so much on my mind and hands at the time that I just didn't have the motivation to continue to search for him. Even though my mom had hopes of finding the son that was taken from her so long ago, she understood where I was coming from and said we could pick up where we left off later on down the line.

Eventually, I had a good talk with Mama Nisa and she encouraged me to continue my search. She offered to help me and my mom in any way that she could, and I appreciated her a lot for that. With her encouragement, my mom and I started looking for

Lace again. We hired a private investigator and the search was easier than we ever thought it would be.

Fortunately, Lace's name was never changed so that's what made it easy. Since he had a record and had been locked up before for auto theft, the private investigator was able to track him down using that. When we found a hit, I flew back to my hometown of Detroit to meet up with him. Initially, Lace was not with the shit and didn't want to hear anything I had to say. He told me to take my ass back where the fuck I came from because he ain't got no family.

Come to find out, after he was snatched from the hospital, Lace was dropped off at a safe haven place and eventually placed into foster care, where he stayed until he maxed out at the age of 18. A few months after our first meeting, he called me up and apologized for how he acted. Since then, we had been keeping in touch and now here he was in the flesh.

"I guess this place ain't as country as I thought it was," he said as he looked around. "How the hell you end up here anyway?"

"I told you it wasn't, and that's a long story that I'm going to have to save for another day," I told him, as we walked back to my truck.

I wasn't going to hit him with the crazy details of my life just

32

yet. We were still fairly new to each other, so I was going to have to ease into that, if I ever felt like sharing that with him. Brother or not, that wasn't just something that I told anyone. It took for the shit to bite me in the ass for me to tell Sire, Ry, and the rest of the goon squad.

"Damn, yo' nigga must take good care of you, huh?" Lace said, while eyeing my Bentley as we walked towards it.

I gave a small smile, but I didn't bother to respond. I hated whenever I thought about Sire because it always made me feel a certain way. I hadn't seen him in two years. I only got a chance to visit him once in prison, before he shut that all the way down. I was so hurt when he called me the next day and told me not to come see him anymore and that he was letting me go.

I was confused and at a loss for words. One minute things were going good between us, then we got hit with the major blow of him being charged with his baby mama's murder, then all of a sudden he was cutting me off. I made a promise that I was going to ride with him no matter what, but he wouldn't even let me live up to that.

No matter how much I tried to hate or be mad at Sire, I couldn't. Even when I tried to go see him because I didn't think he was serious and he just ended up denying my visit, I couldn't find it in my heart to hate him. I had been with Sire long enough to know that he wasn't the average nigga, so whenever he did some off the wall shit, he was using that as a way to cover up for what he was really feeling.

Even though Sire did what he did, I still hadn't turned my back on him. Sire had left some money behind, and I had to dig into it since I wasn't working or in school at the time he was sentenced. After I finished getting my degree, I opened my own event planning business that was doing very well. I replaced every penny I borrowed from Sire, plus interest. I don't know why, but I just had a feeling he was coming back to me. So, I opened him up a Swiss account, as well as the rest of the goon squad, just in case anything else were to happen, they would have access to their money. Every week, I gave Ry or Mama Nisa some money to put on his books. No matter what, I could never just leave him like that.

"Hello?" I answered my ringing phone.

"Aye, lil' sis," Ry's voice came through the phone. "I need you to come pick this money up and you know what to do with it," he said.

That was another thing. I had somehow taken over all of Sire's duties and responsibilities within the operation. That was one thing

I was pretty sure Ry didn't tell his brother, and I couldn't say I was mad about it. The last thing I needed was for Sire to find out that his kids' mother had suddenly turned into something like a trap queen overnight. It's not like it was ever in my plans or dreams to low key be doing this, but shit happens.

"Okay, I'm on my way," I said before hanging up. "You mind taking a ride with me before we head to the house?" I asked Lace.

"Do what you gotta do, I'm just chilling," he said, before slouching in the seat.

With that being said, I changed directions and headed towards the meeting spot, or what the guys liked to call the dungeon.

-$-

Twenty minutes later, I was pulling up to the dungeon, where Ry and Monty were standing outside talking and smoking. I noticed Lace shifted in his seat a little, but I shrugged it off and chopped it up to him being apprehensive around people he doesn't know.

"I'll be right back," I said before getting out the car. "Hey, y'all."

"What up, Lady," Monty spoke with a head nod before taking a toke from his blunt.

"Hold up, who the fuck is that?" Ry questioned with his finger pointed at my passenger's side window, not bothering to return my greeting.

I glanced behind me at Lace, who was just staring at him with a blank expression.

"That's just my brother, Ry, what's—"

"And you brought that nigga here?" he questioned. "You know what's about to go down and you thought it was okay to bring him *here*?" he chastised me.

I shot my eyes over to Monty because I really wasn't understanding why Ryan was tripping right now. He was the one who called me to come pick the money up, but now that I was here, he wanted to go off on me.

"He basically saying that shit ain't safe because we don't know that nigga," Monty chimed in, helping me understand.

"Hell, *you* don't even know that nigga," Ry added.

"It's a problem or something?" I heard from behind me as I heard my car door open.

I turned around to find Lace getting out of the car with a scowl on his face. I glanced back in Ry's direction and could see the vein in the side of his neck sticking out, which was a clear sign that he

36

was pissed off, or slowly getting there.

"Nigga, it will be if you don't get yo' ass back in that damn car," he spat, while throwing his cigarette on the ground. "Who the fuck this bitch ass nigga think he is?" he rhetorically asked, as he leaned off his truck with his hand on his gun.

I stood there stuck because I was confused on what the hell was going on. These two niggas didn't even know each other from a can of paint, but were two seconds away from killing each other.

"Whoa, Lace, let's just go," I said, as I tried to deescalate the situation.

I thought Monty would help or at least be a voice of reason, but that was dead. He was standing right there next to Ry, ready to go to war along with his right-hand man if need be. *This shit is so crazy and unnecessary*, I thought, as I tried to get my brother back in the car.

Without putting up too much of a fight, Lace allowed me to walk him back to the car and we both got in with no words exchanged. I didn't even bother saying anything else to Ryan. My main concern was getting these two away from each other before they could go at each other's throats.

"I don't know who that nigga is and I really don't give a fuck either. I just wasn't feeling the way that he was talking to you. You might be okay with that shit, but I'm not. What the fuck type of brother would I be if I let any nigga come at you crazy? Nah, I'm here now and that shit not gonna fly with me," Lace said as he shook his head.

I didn't even respond for the simple fact that I couldn't. I hadn't been around Lace enough to know how his attitude was or stuff like that, but I could already tell I had something on my hands.

Four – Ry

"I'm going to see my brother Saturday, so I'm going to have to drop her off Friday night, but you know how that goes," I told Tasha as I buckled my daughter in her car seat.

Having Ryley or any child period, grow up in a broken home, was something that I never wanted. Unlike most of my comrades in the hood, I was raised in a household with both of my parents who loved each other and were actually married. Even though Big Reis was a hood nigga to his heart, he was never ashamed to show and declare his love for my mom. They proved to everyone that there was definitely love in the hood, and that's what I wanted.

Unfortunately, shit just didn't quite work out that way. Even though I had mad love for Tasha, I was far from being *in* love with her. Our relationship had run its course long ago, but we have a mutual respect for each other as Ryley's parents, and we were doing the damn thing with this co-parenting shit.

"Got it. So how's Lady doing?" Tasha asked, as she folded her arms and leaned against the car.

Initially, things between Lady and Tasha weren't that good because of their first run in with each other. Tasha used to be wild and off the chain back when we were together, and swore every female I came in contact with I was fucking. She tried to go there with Lady one time, but she shut that down before Tasha could even get started, and things had been real tense between them ever since.

That was until the fellas and I started getting the kids together every other weekend for some family time. The more the two were around each other, the more the tension subsided and they became cool.

"I don't know, I ain't talked to her in a minute," I shrugged.

It had been over two weeks since the incident at the dungeon went down. She hadn't made any efforts to reach out to me, and I damn sure ain't have shit to say about the situation. I felt all of that could've been avoided had Lady just dropped that unknown nigga off somewhere before she came to get the money.

I, as well as the rest of the fellas, don't even know that nigga, so I slightly feel disrespected by the fact that she would even think it was okay to do that stupid shit. There's a time and a place for everything and if she wanted me to meet that nigga, that wasn't the time or the place. We do too much in that damn warehouse, and there's no telling what ideas that nigga would've got, or what he would try to do on some sneaky shit. Then I would be the one responsible for putting a bullet in Lady's long lost brother's head, and everybody knows a nigga like me don't give a fuck.

Tasha slightly turned her head to the side and looked at me funny. "Why not, Ryan? I know you're not still stuck on that stupid sh…stuff that went down," Tasha grilled, as she checked to see if Ryley was listening.

We were trying to watch what we said around her because she was at that age where she was picking things up, and we've heard at least two curse words come out of her mouth before.

"I just ain't had the time; plus, she been so caught up in this new nigga that can't nobody say shit to her," I expressed.

"Cut it out, Ry. You have time to do everything you *want* to do. Besides, he's not just some 'new nigga' as you put it. He's her brother that she just found and she's trying to get to know him. You can't blame her or be mad at her for that. Stop being the asshole that you are, stop being jealous and go talk to her. You two are better than this."

I just shook my head as I tried to figure out when my baby mama started turning into the voice of reason around here. She went from slashing my tires, to giving advice on some real shit. I had to chuckle at that fact because it was crazy how life works. Most niggas' baby mamas be sane before the baby, then crazy after you knock them up. But my situation was reversed. I thank God for

42

Ryley, because she calmed Tasha's ass down…a lot.

"Alright, man, I hear you," I told her, as I leaned down in the car and gave my daughter a kiss.

"I know you can hear me, but that doesn't mean you're listening to me," Tasha said.

"I'm always listening," I said as I gave her a kiss on the forehead. "I'm about to go holla at her right now," I let her know.

"Good. Call and let me know how it goes," Tasha told me as she got in the car.

I just nodded my head and stuffed my hands in my pocket, as I stood there watching them until they were all the way up the street. Once Tasha's car was no longer in my line of vision, I went back into the house to grab a pair of car keys and to lock up.

-$-

Before I could even lift my hand to knock on the front door, it was being swung open and I was greeted by Lady, who had none other than Sire's twin, also known as KJ's, little bad ass attached to her hip. If you didn't know any better, you would swear that Lady pushed him out her own cooch, because she treated him no different than she did the twins.

"What's up, lil' nigga?" I asked, as I ruffled the curly bush at

43

the top of his head.

"Sup, nigga?" he replied back.

"What I tell you about that mouth, Kasire? You want me to pop you?" Lady firmly chastised him.

My nephew just shook his head with a little pout, before laying it on Lady's shoulder. I couldn't do anything but let out a small chuckle because he was definitely his father's son. Sad to say, but Lady surely had something on her hands because KJ was already too much like Sire, and he was only two years old. Wasn't sure if that was a good thing or a bad thing, but what I was sure of was that the world didn't need any more Sires in it.

"My bad, that was all my fault. He just repeating what I said," I told her. "How you know I was here though?" I inquired with a raised brow.

"You must have forgotten I got this high-tech ass security system installed that y'all insisted that I get," Lady said with a roll of her eyes.

It wasn't that the rest of the fellas and I felt as if Lady couldn't protect herself, it was the fact that we weren't about to take the chance of anything happening to her, especially when she had three kids in the house with her. Sire would have no understanding of the situation if he found out that we let anything happen to Lady or one of his. I honestly believed he would do a prison break, just to handle the niggas responsible for touching his family, then come after all of us in the squad for letting the shit go down.

I just nodded my head as I peeked in the house behind her. "You gonna let a nigga in or I gotta stand out here like you don't want me in your shit?"

"Shit!" KJ yelled out.

Lady raised her hand to pop him in his mouth, but I came in with the save by taking him from her arms before she could hit him. I understand what she was going through, because Ryley was doing the same shit. *This terrible twos shit ain't no joke.*

"I wish his damn daddy was here, this shit is so frustrating," Lady mumbled under her breath, as she let out a sigh to show her frustration.

I followed behind her as she walked back into the house, closing the door behind me. Two years after the fact, I never stopped to think about how much stress Lady was actually under by having to raise not one, but three kids by herself. Yea, she may have had help from the rest of us, but the truth of the matter was, she had to do this shit 24/7. On top of that, she hadn't had any contact with Sire since he'd been behind bars.

"Excuse the house, Ry. It's hard to keep it clean when you have to chase behind three toddlers," Lady said, as she started picking toys up across the room.

"Man, chill, Lady. You know I'm not even on that," I told her as I put KJ down in his playpen. "I actually came to talk to you about something," I let her know.

"What's up?"

"That shit that went down."

Lady nodded her head. "Yea, what was up with that? You threw me all the way off with the way you came at me."

"I wasn't necessarily coming at you, Lady," I let her know. "I was mad at the fact that you were being careless. You were so caught up in the fact that you were reunited with this nigga that you brought him to the place that we not only hold our drugs from time to time, we also have shit loads of money there. We kill niggas there and much more. You don't know that nigga and neither do we, so we can't trust that he won't be on some other shit. I know that's your brother, but you can't be moving reckless like that. Get to know that man before you let your emotions get you in a fucked up situation. That's all I was trying to get you to understand," I explained.

Lady and I had been close ever since the day we met back in college. Back then, I really wasn't into that school shit, but I went because Sire thought it would be a safer route for me. When he realized that his little brother was a street nigga to the heart and there wasn't shit a classroom could save me from, he stopped pressuring me into going.

Never would I have imagined that Lady would come into my family and form a soft spot on my brother's cold ass heart. I had only seen that happen once, many, many years ago, but things didn't turn out too well for Sire and the girl, so he's been on some other shit ever since. That was until Lady worked her way in. She's like the sister I never had and I just don't feel right about us beefing or being at odds over some stupid shit.

"I understand that *now*, Ryan, but all you had to do was say that to me then…in a better way. Yes, I was wrong for bringing Lace there and yes, my mind was in another place, but you don't have to be in attack mode about everything. Think about how awkward that shit was and how it made me feel to have both of my brothers about to go at each other's throats over nothing. Regardless of how you feel, Ry, you said you were going to have my back with this Lace situation 100%, so you have to trust me on this. I'm not asking you or the rest of the guys to be his best friend, but at least respect the fact that he is indeed my brother, which makes him my family. He's here and in my life now, but that doesn't mean I love y'all any less. Please, just try to be patient with me on this," Lady stated.

No lie, I was feeling some type of way and you could even say I was a little jealous. For so long I was always the brother, the one there to comfort her, the one protecting her, and there for her when Sire wasn't; the one she came to when she felt like she ain't have no one else. Now, I felt like with her brother being around, all that shit was about to change. You can say I was wrong for feeling the way I do, but I don't want this man fucking up our family dynamic.

"Alright, Lady, you got that. I won't say no more about the nigga, but I need you to let him know trying to step to me like he did ain't a good idea. I'll give him a pass because he didn't know, but it's up to you to let him know from here on out what could possibly happen to him," I warned.

Lady just let out a sigh while playfully rolling her eyes. Even though she was brushing me off, she knew I meant every word I said. Suddenly, the look on her face went from playful to serious, but before I could ask her what was wrong, she spoke.

"Are you going to see him this weekend?" she asked, in reference to me going to see Sire.

I nodded my head in confirmation. "Yea, I'mma leave bright

and early," I told her.

She cleared her throat while moving a piece of her hair behind her ear. Her eyes glanced over at KJ, who was in his own little world in his playpen, before looking back at me.

"Can you tell him that me and the kids love him and we miss him so much."

I tried to ignore the fact that her voice slightly cracked when she said that. I smiled and pulled her in for a kiss, placing a kiss on the top of her head.

"It's going to get better, Lady. I promise it will."

I wasn't too sure if I believed that shit myself, but there was nothing wrong with having a little hope.

Charmanie Saquea

Five – Toine

"Aye, man, hurry yo' ass up!" I yelled with the remote in my hand, ready to press play.

Moments later, I heard feet shuffling before I was met with the sight of my flavor of the month, rushing into the room with a bowl of popcorn. Noel is a cool chick I met at a bar about five months ago. I saw her, I wanted her and being the nigga that I am, I got her. It wasn't anything serious between us and we were just cooling. Besides, I had enough women in my life right now considering all my baby mamas.

Speaking of, when Noel first found out about my kids and their mamas, her first instinct was to run for the hills, and I let her. The one thing I wasn't about to do was chase somebody. If you felt like my kids were going to be a problem for you, then you could get the fuck on because they came before anybody, all seven of them. Yes, seven. Come to find out, Alisha's son was in fact mine and that was proven by the DNA test I took the day he was born.

Of course, that caused some more friction in my relationship with Lala, even though we were already broken up at the time. No matter how much she tried to deny it or act like it didn't faze her, Lala was hoping that I wasn't the baby's father so we could go back to the way we were before this incident even came about. She was fazed so much by the DNA results that she went out and got cozy with a fuck nigga. Seeing *my* Lala with another man was some shit that I just couldn't take, and it fucks me up a little, but I knew I couldn't stop her.

"I had to wait for the popcorn to finish popping," Noel huffed at my rushing her, as she sat on the couch.

She had me watching some dumb ass movie on Netflix, and I was ready to get this shit over with. As soon as I pushed play, my phone started ringing. Low and behold, I sat here and thought one of my baby mamas up.

"Yo," I answered.

"Open the door," Lala said, then hung up before I could respond.

I just shook my head and got up to open the door for her worrisome ass. Things between Lala and I are very bipolar. One day we can be good and getting along just fine, then the next day we were at each other's throats and shit.

"Really?" Noel asked, and I just ignored her.

When I opened the door, I walked outside and watched as Lala climbed out of her truck, compliments of me. I couldn't help but to lick my lips at the itty bitty ass romper she had on that had her thick thighs on display and barely covered her ass. Even after having two kids, my baby mama was the shit.

"Yo' nigga let you come out the house with that shit on?" I asked when she got closer.

She looked down at her outfit then back up to me like she ain't know what I was talking about.

"What's wrong with what I got on?" she questioned.

"This," I said, cuffing her ass. "You got this shit hanging all out and nine times out of ten you ain't got no fucking panties on," I fussed.

"Move, Toine." She swatted my hand away from her ass cheek. "And I do have panties on. It's called a thong, thank you very much," she said, pushing past me.

"You know I wouldn't dare let you wear no bullshit like this out the house. You pull shit like this with him 'cause he a fuck nigga with no authority," I told her.

Lala just waved me off dismissively before barging her ass in my house.

"Probably ain't even hitting the pussy right," I mumbled.

It must not have been low enough though, because Lala looked back and cut her eyes at me. I just shrugged. She didn't even bat an eye or care about the fact that Noel was sitting on the couch. She ignored the fuck out of her as she made her way to the kitchen. I shook my head at her as I followed behind her.

"That was rude as fuck, Alani," I said before biting my lip, as I rubbed my dick against her soft ass.

"Uh, no, what's rude is you pushing up on me while you got a bitch in there on your couch and when you know I got a man. Back up," she pushed me.

I let out a small chuckle as I backed up a little and watched her go in my freezer and come out with a Popsicle before opening it and putting it in her mouth. I had to grab my dick and readjust it because the way she was sucking on that Popsicle was bringing back some very fond memories for me. When Lala looked up and noticed what I was up to, she took the Popsicle out of her mouth and scrunched her face up at me.

"You are so nasty. Get your mind right." She rolled her eyes.

"Aye, let me put another one in you," I said with a straight face.

"Antoine, I'm not about to…" Her voice trailed off and she

placed her hand lightly on my neck. "You got it redone?" she said softly.

I didn't bother to respond, as she continued to run her fingers over the spot on my neck where I got her name tattooed when we were teenagers. Everybody thought I was crazy as hell when I got 'Alani' tattooed on the side of my neck in a basement, but I knew what the fuck I was doing. I knew she was going to be the woman I was going to spend the rest of my life with. Then two weeks later, we found out she was pregnant with AJ.

"Toine, I…oh, I'm sorry." I heard Noel's voice from behind me, but my eyes never left Lala.

I saw something flash through her eyes, but it was quick and I couldn't catch it. She tried to back up and remove her hand, but I caught it and took her hand in mine.

"Toine, don't," she shook her head.

"Don't what?"

"I didn't come here for this," she said as she softly snatched her hand away. "I came to talk but I didn't know you had company. I'll come—"

"You'll say what you got to say now and get off that bullshit."

"Anyway," she rolled them funky ass eyes again. "Your son

wants to play football, but I told him that I would talk to you about it first."

"What's wrong with him playing football?" I asked with my face scrunched up.

"Do you think that's a safe sport? I don't…"

I didn't mean to, but I burst into laughter when she said that. Obviously, Lala didn't find anything funny, so she was looking at me like I was crazy.

"La, Junior is a grown ass man, he's going to be alright. If he gets hit, oh well. It's not like he's going to lay on the field and cry. *You* might cry but he won't."

I ducked just in time because Lala's fist came right at me.

"You play too much. I am not going to cry. Anyway, that's all I wanted. I guess I'll get going now."

"Hold up," I said as I reached in my pocket.

"Wh…what you doing?" Lala mumbled as she eyed the bills in my hand.

"Here," I said instead of answering her question.

"This for the kids, right?" she asked, as she examined the wad of money I had just practically shoved in her hand.

I shook my head because she was playing it crazy. "The kids already got their money from me. This is for you. Stop playing with me, Alani."

"Antoine, I—"

"Look, fuck all that extra shit. If yo' nigga got a problem with me giving the mother of my kids some money, tell him to come see me. From the first day I laid eyes on you, I told you I had you and that I was going to take care of you. That shit not going to change just because you decided you wanna pass the time with this lame ass nigga. I told you once before but I'll say it again, I'll let you do whatever you feel you need to do to come to your senses and realize that me and you are never going to be over, but don't take too fucking long, Alani."

Without saying anything, Lala just sighed before throwing the money in her bag and making her exit out of the kitchen. That was cool with me because I really didn't want to hear whatever might have come out of her mouth anyway. Lala and I both knew that her heart belonged to me, and the only reason she was even entertaining this other nigga was to get her point across.

Little did she know, shit like that didn't mean shit to me because I was still going to do what I wanted to do when it came to her. The only reason I hadn't imposed on their so called relationship yet was because I was letting her think she was doing something, but Lala was going to always be mine. No nigga was going to ever be able to take my place, just like no bitch could ever take hers.

Six – Sire

"What's up, Tracy?" I asked as I took my seat.

Tracy had been working hard and busting her ass for the past two years since I've been locked up, to get me out of here. It damn near broke her heart when she wasn't able to beat my case and she promised me that she wasn't going to rest until I was a free man again.

"I did it, Si," she beamed proudly. "I told you I was going to—"

"Hold up, Tracy. Don't fucking play with me right now. Get the fuck out of here."

I wasn't trying to be rude, but I wasn't about to sit up here and play with my freedom. Even though it was some bullshit and I didn't agree with it, it was already determined that I was going to be spending the rest of my life in this fucking hell hole, so I wasn't about to get my hopes up right now.

"I'm serious, Kasire. I wouldn't have even came all the way up here and brought this to you if I wasn't sure that you were going home."

I looked deep into her eyes and I saw that she was desperate for me to believe her. I sat back in my seat and ran my hands down my beard before running them over my now bald head that I had adopted since being locked up. Gone were my seasick waves and now I was rocking a freshly shaved head from the barbershop in the prison.

"How?" was all I wanted to know.

"Well, it comes to find out that the DA was hiding evidence for the case at his house. He, along with his police officer friends that arrested you, had been investigating you and the guys for a while. They were so hell bent on catching you slipping so they could lock at least one, if not all of you up. It's like he had some sort of personal vendetta against you and you never had an idea. Apparently, his assistant couldn't take it anymore and started telling all the business. Also, the judge is in hot water as well because he took a bribe to sentence you," Tracy explained.

I sat there speechless because I really didn't know what to say. This whole time I was being set the fuck up and never even knew the shit. The more I sat there and thought about it, the more my blood started to boil. Since being locked up, I had tried to work on keeping that crazy muthafucka inside of me that was ruthless and didn't give a fuck about anyone or anything, but shit like this is what brought him out.

If it was one thing besides my family that I didn't play about, it was definitely my freedom, and these sons of bitches had fucked with both. I had missed out on two, damn near three years of my kids' life, all because of a hard on some bitch made niggas had for me. All this time I was thinking it was just a misunderstanding, but the whole time it was a setup against my black ass to get me off the streets for good.

"Who else knows this?" I asked.

"I haven't told Toine yet, if that's what you're asking. The only people who know this bit of information is me and the people who are doing the investigation. The judge, the DA, and the arresting officers are all in some major trouble and facing criminal charges," she told me.

"I want you to give the information on every muthafucka who had something to do with me getting locked up to Toine. Tell him to sit tight and don't make any moves until I touch down. I don't want anyone besides him knowing that I'm getting out, understood?"

Tracy paused and gave me a knowing look. She had known me long enough to know what I was thinking and what I planned on having done to everyone who played a part in doing me wrong. I had been gone away from the streets for too long, and since these muthafuckas wanted Sire so bad, they were going to get him.

Tracy nodded her head before shifting in her seat.

"I can do that for you. Anything else you need me to do?"

I just shook my head to let her know there wasn't anything else that she could do for me. She had already done way more that than I expected from her.

-$-

Later on that night in my cell, Lady was weighing heavily on my mind. It wasn't uncommon for me to think about her but for some reason, tonight she was pulling on me like crazy. It was crazy to me how Lady had just walked into my life unexpectedly, and I haven't been able to shake her ass since.

We've had plenty of downs in our relationship, probably more than we've had ups. I've never had someone that was able to handle my crazy ass like she can. Hell, even Lexus's trifling ass couldn't take it, so she jumped on the next nigga's dick at the first chance she got. Lady though, she's my little rider. No matter how many times she claimed to be done with me or said she didn't want shit to do with me, she was always there when I needed her the most.

Shifting in this raggedy ass thing they called a bed, I reached in the slit in my mattress and pulled out my cell phone. Nobody knew I had this but my brother since he was the one responsible for getting it to me. Unconsciously, I dialed a number and waited for an answer. The phone rang about four times and just when I was about to hang up, the sweetest thing I ever heard played in my ears.

"Hello?" Lady answered.

My heart rate sped up and it was damn near about to beat out of my chest when I heard her voice. It had been over two years since I saw her or heard her voice, and I hadn't even realized how much I missed her until tonight.

"Hello?" she repeated, but yet, I still didn't say anything.

I could hear my kids in the background causing chaos, and it pained me that I wasn't there with them. I heard a gasp come from Lady's mouth as if she recognized who was on the other end.

"Sire?" she questioned as if she wasn't sure. "I love you."

A small smile spread across my face before I removed the phone from my ear and ended the call. I quickly went to my settings and blocked her number so she wouldn't try to call me back. I rolled back over and put the contraband back in its rightful hiding place, as satisfaction filled my body.

Just hearing her voice was good enough to hold me over until I was able to hold her in my arms again.

"I love you, too, baby girl," I whispered before closing my eyes.

Tonight, I was going to have sweet dreams with my girl on my mind. I was slowly counting down the days until I was able to get my family back.

Charmanie Saquea

Seven – Monty

The bass from the speakers flowed through my body, as I sat low in my seat watching her like I was stalking my prey. I hadn't taken my eyes off of her since I walked in the ratchet ass club almost two hours ago. I just found out on accident three days ago that the mother of my child was working at a club on one of the most dangerous sides of town. The exact same side of town I did most of my dirt.

I sat up in my seat when I noticed the same nigga that was smiling all in her face earlier was back again, but this time he was a little too close for my liking. He had his hand all on Cola's waist, just barely touching her ass and if I didn't know any better, I would think she was liking the shit.

My jaw and trigger finger both started twitching at the same time, as I watched him lean in and whisper something in her ear that caused a smile that was damn near a mile long to spread across her lips. It was over for his ass, though, when he placed a soft but sensual kiss on her ear. I jumped up while reaching behind me for my gun that I always kept on me.

Just like the red sea, the crowd parted when everyone noticed the murderous look on my face. It was no secret of who I was, who

I rolled with, and what we were about. Niggas knew that if you saw at least one of us, shit was about to get crazy, but if you saw all of us together, shit was about to get out of control. Muthafuckas thought just because our nigga, Sire, was down for the count at the moment, that we were going to lay low and be hurting. We may have been hurting, but that shit just made us go harder than we ever went.

I cocked my gun as I got closer to Cola and it was as if she could finally sense that her life was in danger, because she looked up like a deer caught in the headlights, trying to figure out what was going on. When she finally realized it was me, a look of horror came across her face.

"Bear, no!" she yelled, but it was too late.

I already had my gun pointed at him and let one loose on his ass.

POW!

The little ugly muthafucka must've had an angel on his shoulder or something because he ducked out of the way in time. Even so, I was still on his ass, and if it was one thing he couldn't do, he couldn't out run me. Before he could even get away good, I snatched his ass back and knocked him over the head with the butt of my gun, causing him to fall like a sack of potatoes.

"Come here, lil' bitch," I spat, as I continued my assault on his face.

"Monty, that's enough!" I heard Cola yell, but I tuned her out as my gun continued to pummel into his face. "Monty...MONTANA, I SAID STOP!"

Suddenly, I stopped when I felt a stinging sensation on the left side of my face. As if I was in some sort of trance, I slowly turned my head towards Cola and that's when I realized she had just slapped me. I stood up and walked in her direction. She backed up with a look of fear on her face as if she was scared that I was going to hit her ass back or something. Even though I should have, she knew better than that

"Let's go," I said through clenched teeth.

Without putting up a fuss or a fight, Cola followed behind me as I led the way out of the hole in the wall of a club. There was no movement in the club and all eyes were definitely on us, as everyone tried to figure out just what I was going to do with Cola.

"Monty—"

"Get in the fucking car, Nicola!" my voice boomed when we reached the parking lot.

I didn't want to hear shit she had to say right now. At the

moment, the safest thing for her to do would be for her to get in her car and drive to her house where we could try to have a decent conversation. Rolling her eyes, she did as she was told. I stood there with my chest puffing out as I tried to control my anger and my breathing, because it was taking everything in me not to put my hands on that damn girl.

After standing there and watching her pull out of the parking lot, I finally made my way to my car and jumped in. I ran my hands down my face to try to help me calm down, but it seemed the shit wasn't working. The shit I saw back in that club had me so bent out of shape that it was crazy. Only Cola had the power to make a nigga feel this way. Figuring that I sat there long enough, I burned rubber as I made my way out of the parking lot.

I broke every traffic law imaginable as I sped to Cola's house. I knew that it was going to be a very long night for us, and the sooner we could get to this bullshit, the better. When I got to her house, I saw that her car was parked in the driveway and I was happy that she didn't try to pull no slick little bullshit like going to pick Nylah up from wherever she was so I couldn't get in her ass tonight, because that wouldn't have done shit but further pissed me off.

"Bring yo' stupid ass here!" I yelled as soon as I walked in the house, slamming the door behind me.

"I'm tired of you disrespecting me, Montana!" she had the nerve to say, as she stomped in the room.

"Disrespecting you?" I asked indignantly. "Let's not talk about disrespect. Disrespect is that shit you pulled with that half dead ass nigga at that sorry ass club tonight. Crazy thing about it is you thought you was low and slick because you didn't even know I was there tonight, and you almost got away with the shit too," I spat.

"I wasn't trying to be low about anything, Monty. I'm single; I can do what I want to do. You don't want me, remember?"

I almost knocked Cola's ass into another generation when she said that bullshit. Now she was playing mind games and I didn't have time for the bullshit she was trying to pull.

"Fuck out of here, Nicola! You're the one who was doing all that yelling about how you didn't want to be with me because I was in the streets, but you didn't have a problem with me paying for your tuition when you wanted to go to school to be a physical therapist. Guess what? That shit was paid for with my street money. You don't have a problem driving that Beamer paid for by my street money. You don't have a problem riding or slurping this dick damn near every day. Guess what, baby? It's attached to a street nigga," I told her, as I grabbed my dick so she could get the message.

"You are so fucking ignorant, Montana, that it's sad. I don't give a fuck about none of that shit!" she yelled. "Since you wanted to bring it up, let's set the shit straight since you like to brag about what you do for me. Not one time did I ask you to pay my tuition for me. You did that because you said you were proud that I was finally doing what I said I always wanted to do, and you refused to let me get a loan when you had the money. Smart ass. Also, I never asked you for that car outside. You gave that to me because you said you didn't want me and your daughter taking public transportation. I was fine catching the bus and I have no problem doing it again. Another thing, nigga. You're not the only nigga with a dick. You act like I need you or something. That's the main reason I went out and got a job because I knew I couldn't depend on your stupid ass for too much longer. You can get the fuck on because I don't need you to do shit for me. Nylah and I are gone be straight regardless," Cola ranted.

I walked up on her and glared down at her. We were so close that I could feel her heart that was about to beat out of her chest. It was no secret that I loved Cola. I loved her so much that I hated her little ass sometimes. Whether she knew it or not, it hurt me that she refused to accept that fact that she fell in love with a street nigga. The streets are all I know and the streets are what basically raised me.

I didn't have a father in my life, so like most kids that grew up in the hood, I turned to the streets to guide me and teach me. Cola knew who and what I was when she first met me, so the fact that she chose all these years later to complain about some shit that she knew was never going to change, had me looking at her differently. If she had such a problem with me being in the streets, I honestly feel as if she never should've brought her ass back to Richmond.

"Cool, you win. Don't call me, text me, or none of that shit unless it has something to do with Nylah. I don't give a fuck if your car breaks down in the middle of the road in the valley of the shadow of death; don't call my shit. Since my thugged out ass ain't never gonna be good enough for you," I spat, before walking away.

It seemed as if I was always going out of my way to accommodate Cola or make sure she was straight, but all she did was spit in my face in return. She only loved my thuggish ways when it was convenient for her, or if she could get what she wanted. But the moment she realized shit wasn't all glitter and gold, she wanted to fold and bail out on me.

After tonight though, I was really done with Cola. If she couldn't accept me for who I really was, then there was no point in us trying to fake a bullshit ass relationship. She was going to realize how good she had it with me and that there's no nigga on this earth that's ever going to love and protect her like I will. By the time she does, I'll be with the girl who appreciates me…all of me.

Eight – Lady

I finished tying up my black Timberland boots before looking in the mirror at my appearance. Nodding my head in approval, I made my way to the closet and keyed in the code to the safe that Sire kept it there. When it popped open, I reached in the back for his twin desert eagles he kept locked away.

I checked the clip to make sure it was full before making sure the safety was on and placing them behind me in the waistline of my pants. I unzipped the two duffle bags that I had hidden under my bed, and ran my hands over the neatly stacked bills in there. Making sure everything was good, I closed it back up.

I had to chuckle at the fact that I went from being a thug's wife to a damn thug myself. I knew there would be some serious problems if Sire knew what I was doing in his absence, but I had to make sure my family was straight. I never imagined or planned on him being locked up. It threw us for a loop, so it fell on me to pick up the pieces.

Like I did every time I made a move, I got down on one knee and said a quick, but silent, prayer.

God, I ask that you just watch over me. You know my heart and you know I mean well, so let no weapon formed against me prosper so that I can make it back home to my babies. Amen.

"What you doing?" I heard from behind me, scaring the hell out of me.

I jumped up to find Lace leaning in the doorway of my bedroom, eating a peach. I was still trying to adjust to the fact that he was living here with me for the time being. He had this little habit of where he liked to sneak up on you without making noise, and the shit irritated the hell out of me.

So far, things between us were cool. I quickly learned that Lace was definitely not a people person. I tried to get him to come out and do things with the rest of the guys so he could at least make some friends here in Richmond, but he deaded that idea and told me to never bring it back up. I don't know if his little run in with Ryan the first day he got here had anything to do with it or not, but he wasn't too thrilled about making new friends.

One thing I will give him though, is he's good with kids. KJ and Little Man, as I like to call Kasim, they love him. Even my diva, Kasmira, warmed up to him right away and she was like her daddy when it came to meeting new people.

"I thought y'all were at Chuck E. Cheese," I said, pulling my shirt down in the back to hide my guns.

"Fuck Chuck E," he said before taking another bite of his peach. "Don't ignore my question though. What you doing?" he said with his mouth full, while eyeing me suspiciously.

"Nothing, Lace. I have to make a run real quick though," I told him, hoping he would drop it and leave me alone.

Sometimes he took this brother thing a little too far. I'm not sure if it was because I grew up as an only child or what, but I was having a hard time getting used to this having a brother. Often times whenever he would see that I was going somewhere, he would ask me where I was going, who I was going with, how long I was going to be gone and all that. He claims it was because he was making sure I was safe and he just wanted to protect me, but I couldn't tell if he was my nigga or my brother.

Right now, there was no way in hell I could tell him where I was going and what I was about to do. I learned from the last time Ryan cussed me out, I wasn't letting Lace or anybody else for that matter know about our business affairs.

"Hmm, if I were you, I would wear a looser jacket if you're trying to conceal those guns you got on you. Also, never shit where you sleep. You never know what could happen, gangstress." He winked before turning around and walking away from my bedroom door.

With my face pulled into a semi scowl, I turned around and looked in my full body mirror. When I saw that you could see the gun, I shrugged and took off the jacket I had on, and switched to a looser and slightly longer one like Lace suggested.

-$-

"Welcome, mami. You got that for me?" Amilio asked.

Amilio was this Dominican dude that I found out the goon squad did business with. One thing I can say is that Sire did a pretty good job of keeping his street life away from our home. Besides that one little incident with Gerard, or should I say Drill, I've never really seen any of his street dealings. As far as the little situation with Drill trying to kill me, I guess you can say that one was really my fault because I was fraternizing with the enemy and didn't even know it until it was too late.

As far as his drug business, Sire never said shit and I never asked shit. I wasn't stupid by a long shot. I knew what he was into and what he was about when I first laid eyes on him, but like I said, that life and his life with me never really met. Now, here I was jumping into *his* world head first.

"Only if you got that for me," I said, referring to the drugs.

"You can have whatever you want, mami. I do mean

whatever." He smiled a slick, but seductive, smile.

Whenever I was in Amilio's presence, he made it a point to flirt with me and never tried to hide the fact that he wanted me. Ryan and the rest of the guys painted him as this ruthless ass man that played no games and would have no problems putting a bullet in my head if I stepped out of line. When, I first laid eyes on Amilio, I didn't even know he was who they were talking about.

He stood about six feet even, smooth skin that had a peanut butter complexion to it, light brown eyes that were hooded by long eyelashes that naturally curled. He had long, wavy hair that he kept in a ponytail. All bullshit aside, he was sexy as hell but I would never cross that line. I had a man, even if he wasn't my man at the moment.

I could see Ryan's jaw and fists flexing out the corner of my eye. I could tell that he didn't appreciate the shit that Amilio was trying to pull. I had grown so accustomed to the shit that it didn't bother or faze me anymore.

"Just the drugs, please, thank you," I said with a fake smile plastered on my face.

Amilio waved his right hand in the air and one of his little henchmen walked over to collect the bags, but I didn't budge. I peered around his big ass and glared at Amilio.

"Not until I see my shit, don't play," I told him.

"Umm, spicy. I like that," Amilio smiled. "Juno, the truck," he ordered his man.

Juno, his henchman that was standing in front of me, let out a low growl like he had a problem following a simple order, and I shot his ass a look that let him know he wasn't putting fear anywhere in my body. I moved to go with him, but of course, Amilio had other plans.

"Ryan, why don't you go with him to check out the product," he said.

"Nah, I'm straight. Lady can handle it," Ry said dryly.

"I have no doubts that she can, but here's the thing. I wasn't asking you to go, I was telling you."

"Well—"

"Ry," I cut him off from the verbal lashing that I just knew was about to come out of his mouth. "Just go, I'll be alright." I rubbed my back to let him know that I was strapped.

Ryan huffed and bit his lip to let me know he wasn't feeling this shit, but he was trusting my judgment on it. I had no doubts about Amilio being a very powerful man and I've heard plenty of stories about how he's actually sent people's body parts to their mama's house, and I wasn't trying to have Ry or I in that predicament.

With the way that Ry's mouth and anger was set up, we wouldn't make it out of this bitch alive. Even though the guys had taken me to the gun range and I had shot my gun plenty of times, I still hadn't shot an actual person yet.

"Lady, Lady, Lady," Amilio said as he rubbed his goatee.

"That's my name," I told him.

He let out a little chuckle as he got up from his seat. "You're so sexy," he said as he leaned up against the table with his arms folded. "So, Sire's never coming home, eh?" he questioned as if he was amused.

I cocked my head to the side and looked at him through the slits in my eyes. "What makes you think that?"

"You need someone that's going to take care of you and your kids. It's two of them, right? With a man like me, you'll never want for anything. A woman like you deserves to be taken care of. I'm pretty sure Sire wasn't getting the job done," he said, as he walked up on me, a little too close for comfort.

I was sure that Amilio had all types of women throwing themselves at him—why wouldn't he? Not only was he sexy, he had the money and the power to go along with his looks. You could tell that he wasn't used to being told no or turned down, but I don't know how many times I had to assure him that this was one pussy he would never be able to taste or feel.

I was a lot of things, but a hoe was nowhere on the list. I would never stoop so low as to sleep with someone that my baby daddy does business with. I'm way too loyal for that shit. Even if Sire never comes home or we never work out, Amilio would never be on my mind.

"No thank you, Amilio. I'm just here to do a job, nothing more. I'm not interested in all the extra shit," I said, trying to be as nice as I could.

"You—"

"Muthafucka, no means no!" I heard Ryan's voice roar before I could even see his face.

"Ryan, it's okay. Everything check out?" I asked, changing the subject so he wouldn't go off.

Instead of answering me, Ryan stood there glaring at Amilio while Amilio just looked at him with a sly smirk, before he let out a small snicker. I knew that didn't do shit but further infuriate Ry because he knew he couldn't kill him. Amilio was their only option at getting money right now in the streets.

"Ryan!" I said a little louder this time. "Did everything check out?" I asked again.

"Yea, it's good," he said, flexing his jaw.

Turning my attention back to Amilio and what I liked to call his watchdog, I tossed the two duffle bags full of money at Juno's feet. It was something about him that I didn't like and I didn't even bother to try to hide my disdain for him.

"Nice doing business with you. Until next time," I smirked, as I turned to make my exit with Ry right behind me.

As soon as we got outside, Ry wasted no time expressing how he felt about Amilio.

"That bitch ass nigga got one more time to cross the line and I'mma fry his wetback ass," he spat with fury.

The vein bulging out the side of his neck was a clear sign that Ryan was pissed off. I couldn't even be mad at him. Not only was Amilio being disrespectful towards me, but he was being disrespectful towards Sire who wasn't even here to defend himself. And that was something that Ryan just couldn't take.

"Don't stress it, Ry. I'm not even sweating him. The shit he says goes right in one ear and out the other." I waved it off.

84

"That may be true, Lady, but that nigga knows he wouldn't be pulling that shit if Sire was out. Then he got the nerve to take shots at my brother like he not one of the main reasons his gay looking ass is making money."

The only thing I could do was shrug because Ry had a point. We both knew that Amilio wouldn't dare be pulling this shit if Sire was out, but on the other hand, *I* wouldn't even be in this shit if Sire was out.

I had no choice but to play nice with Amilio but also let him know that there was never going to be anything between us. I didn't want to be the reason the guys had to cut all ties with him, or start any unnecessary drama. I was trying to avoid the conversation Ry was going to have to have with his brother, if Sire found out the reason they had to find a new connect was because his baby mama came in and fucked shit up.

Charmanie Saquea

Nine – Toine

"What you said this nigga name was?" I asked Ry as I sat up in my chair.

Ry had called a meeting to discuss a nigga who came to him about doing business with him. He let us know that he wasn't going to give him an answer until he talked to us about it. I didn't mind doing business with the cat as long as his money was right, but I still wanted to check his ass out before we went ahead with anything.

"D-Low," Ry answered.

"Never heard of him. He small time?" I questioned.

"From what he told me, he just moved here a little over a year ago. That's all I know so far. I really wasn't trying to discuss business with his ass in public, so I ain't really get no details," he answered.

"You talked to Si about this?" Monty asked.

When Monty brought up Sire, my mind instantly went to the conversation I had with Tracy a few days ago.

Tracy had called me into her office because she said she had something important that she wanted to talk to me about. Not thinking twice, I rushed over to see what the problem was, thinking it had something to do with our daughter, Amaya.

"Hey, Toine, thanks for coming," she said as she closed her office door.

"No doubt, you good? Maya good?" I questioned as I took a seat.

"Yea, we're good. Your daughter is a mess, but I called you here for something else," she said, as she handed me a piece of paper. "I was told to give this to you."

I looked over the paper confused as hell because the only thing that was on it were names and addresses. One of the names stuck out to me as the name of the judge that sentenced Sire, but that was it.

"What's this?"

"I went to see Sire. He's coming home, very soon as a matter of fact. These are the names of all the people who had a hand in locking him up. Sire was set up by everyone on that piece of paper in your hand. He told me to give it to you and for you to sit on it until he gets home. He wants you to be the only one to know when he's coming home and to pick him up when that day comes, so I'll keep you informed," Tracy explained to me.

I didn't have to ask any more questions after that. Sire was my right-hand man, so I knew the moves he was planning to make with this information. He was plotting on them and he wanted me to know.

"Got it. Thanks, Tracy," I said as I stood up.

"No need to thank me. I'm just doing my job," she smiled.

I reached into my pocket and pulled out a wad of money. Pulling off a few bills, I placed them on her desk. Tray went to protest, but I stopped her before she could. I always broke off my kids' mother with some money whenever I saw them. It was just something that I had to do. Even though Tracy was married and her husband liked to help out with Amaya, and I respected him for that, I still gave her money for our daughter whenever I saw fit.

"Toine," she stopped me before I could walk out her office. "Be safe, big head."

"Always," I smiled before walking out.

"Yea, Sire said he was going to trust our judgement on this one."

Even though Sire was locked up, we never excluded him from anything that regarded our business affairs. We let him in on everything that we had going on; everything except for the fact that we had Lady taking over where he left off.

That was a decision that Ry, Monty, and I all made together. We knew Lady wasn't dumb when it came to the street shit, especially considering her past of finessing niggas. We needed a fourth person because Amilio was on some bullshit, talking about the deal he made with us was to work with four people, not three, so he was going to end our business relationship. It was always something about that muthafucka that I didn't like, but I never spoke my piece on it.

So in order to keep the funky ass connect we had, we had to bring somebody quickly. There was nobody else that we really trusted besides Lady, so she was our next best thing besides Sire. We knew if that nigga ever found out what we had Lady doing, he would try to kill us all. That's why we kept this shit to ourselves. Now that he was coming home, we didn't have to worry about it anymore.

"Alright, call him up and set up an appointment for us to meet this nigga. I wanna feel his ass out, then we can go from there," I told Ry.

He nodded his head and said he was going to get right on it.

-$-

Baby Mama From Hell #2: *I'm tired of you ignoring me Antoine. Let's see if you ignore the child support people!*

I had to bite my lip and let out a sinister chuckle as I read the text message Alisha's stupid ass had sent me. Here I was trying to handle business, and she wanted to be on some bullshit. The fact that she was even threatening me with that child support bullshit had me ready to snap her fucking neck. I thought I had gotten rid of my crazy ass baby mama when Heaven's ass went into hiding, but I ended up with another one with Alisha.

This bitch was worse than Heaven ever was though. The only thing Heaven did was throw tantrums when I wouldn't break her off with some dick, but she never threatened me with child support because she knew I took damn good care of my kids. The moment the DNA results came back, revealing that I was indeed her son's father, somehow, this bitch turned into a completely different person.

She thought just because we had a child together that I was supposed to be with her. I had five other baby mamas in this world and was with neither of them, so how she came to that conclusion, I don't know. The moment I told her I didn't want to be with her, which she already knew, her ass started being on some other shit.

Just as I was about to text her ass back, Ry said some shit that stopped me.

"There that nigga go right there."

I'll cuss her ass out later, I thought before I slid my phone in my pocket and looked up.

"Get the fuck outta here," I spat when I saw who it was.

Ry and Monty looked at me with confused looks as I kept my eyes trained on Darius as he sat at the table. This nigga had this big ass façade going on like he was a nine to five ass nigga and had a good career. But the whole time, he was a no good ass street nigga like all the rest of us. I knew I didn't like his ass for a reason.

"You know him?" Monty asked.

"Do I?" I retorted. "This the nigga Lala call herself being in a relationship with," I informed them.

Darius just sat there as if he wasn't even fazed by the fact that he had been lying to Lala since he met her, and that pissed me off. Ry started pulling on his beard. He knew that since I put them on to that little bit of information that shit was about to change. Nobody but me knew who Lala was dating because she never brought his soft ass around.

"So, I'm taking it that she doesn't know?" Ry assumed.

"Nah," Darius answered. "She doesn't know. I keep this part of my life away from my personal life," he said.

I had to laugh even though the shit wasn't funny, because this nigga sounded dumb as hell. There was no such thing as keeping the two separated when you lived the street life, because the shit was eventually going to find its way to your front door. I would know. I was telling myself that same lie until Drill's bitch ass thought it was okay to shoot up my house with my kids and Lala in it. That was the day that I realized that no matter how much I tried to keep them from my street dealings, the shit would always follow me no matter where I went.

Ry looked over at me and I could see the wheels in his head turning before he leaned over to speak to me. "I ain't know this was him. I don't know if it's beef between y'all or not. I'm letting this one be your call. Whatever you wanna do with this situation is up to you. Monty and I stand behind you 100%."

I nodded my head in respect. I just sat there staring at Darius as I thought about what I was going to do. The fact that he had been lying to Lala about who he really was and what he really did for a living, didn't sit right with me. I may have done a lot of things wrong when it came to Lala and I, but one thing I never did to her was lie. I may have withheld some information from her until I figured out how I wanted to tell her, but I never lied about who I

93

was.

From day one, Lala knew I was a street nigga. I never tried to hide that shit from her or anybody else. So, the fact that I knew Lala would be hurt if she found out was rubbing me the wrong way. She did all this talking about how she ended up with a nigga that was different from me, only to end up with one that was just like me. *Ain't that some shit.*

"When Alani finds out, because she will, don't put my name in shit. You just better make sure don't shit happen to her or my kids because you wanna be on some sneaky shit, lying and all that, because if it does…I got a bullet that stays in the chamber just for yo' ass," I let him know.

"We all do," Monty assured him.

Darius just nodded his head like he understood where I was coming from, and I surely hoped he did, because I wasn't about to play with his ass. If anything were to happen to Lala *again*, or my kids. I was going to make sure they would never be able to find his body.

Ten – Sire

Two years, six months, and fourteen days.

After all that time, a nigga was finally free. Even though I should've been happy and filled with joy, that wasn't the case, because I still had business I had to take care of. As bad as I wanted to run home to my girl and kids, I wasn't going to rest until I had the head of every muthafucka that had a hand in getting me locked up for some bullshit.

"Kasire muthafuckin' Lewis."

I couldn't contain the smile on my face even if I wanted to, as I made my way to my best friend. Just like I knew he would after getting my message, Toine was right here to get me. When I made it over to him, he pulled me into a brotherly embrace.

"Nigga, if I didn't know no better I would think that you missed me," I laughed.

"I ain't gon' lie, hell yea I did. Shit just wasn't the same without you, nigga. I'm happy you're back though," he said.

I couldn't even front, I had missed my niggas, too. This wasn't my first time being locked up, but it was the first time I was actually innocent. I was back though, and it was time to let muthafuckas know that you can't keep a real boss down. It was time I made the streets bleed.

"Tracy give you that paper?" I asked him once we got settled in his car.

"She did," he nodded his head. "So what you got planned?"

"Murder," was all I said.

Playtime was officially over. I had sat in prison long enough, thinking and plotting about what I was going to do to everyone when I got out. Now it was time for me to put my plans in motion.

"Where you headed? You need something?" he questioned.

"Nah, I got everything I need at the hideout spot. I'll be staying there until I'm done doing what I need to do."

He took his eyes off the road for a second and looked at me like he wanted to say something, but he opted out instead.

"What?" I asked.

"You not about to go see Lady and the kids?" he asked.

I sat my head back on the seat and thought about if I should go see them or not. I was anxious as hell to see them, but I knew that once I got around them, I wasn't going to want to leave them. And I wouldn't be any good to them because my body would be with them, but my mind wouldn't.

"I gotta take care of business first. You know better than anybody else how I get when I'm on a mission, and I don't need to hurt them any more than I already have, especially Lady. When I'm back with her, I want to be all about her and my kids, with no distractions," I answered.

Toine nodded his head as if he understood where I was coming from. "Respect. You know if you need anything, all you gotta do is ring my line and I'm there."

"Yea, I know. But this is some shit I need to handle by myself. You know any other time I would want my niggas riding out with me, but this is some personal shit," I let him now.

"I understand, nigga. Just do what you gotta do and get back home to your girl and kids. I can't even begin to tell you how much they miss you. One thing I will tell you though, if you ever had doubts about Lady before, get rid of them shits now. That girl is really down for you and your rider. She really held shit down on the outside, even when you told her not to. That girl is A-1," Toine told me.

I couldn't do anything but smile, because he wasn't telling me shit that I didn't already know; he was just confirming my thoughts. I had plans to pay back Lady in the best way possible, for staying true to a nigga even when she didn't have to. Had any other bitch been in her position, they would've folded on me. I had plans for her that I'm sure would make her happy.

-$-

The time on the dashboard read 3:15am. I had just pulled up to the address that belonged to the judge and I couldn't wait to take out my revenge. From what I learned, he was 50 years old, divorced, and living by himself. His wife left him over eight years ago because he had a real bad drinking problem and she got tired of him after years of putting up with his shit.

If he thought his life was going downhill before, he really fucked up when he made the decision to cross me with his comrades. He would've been better off drinking himself into a fucking coma than crossing me; but since he chose the latter, I was going to end his life for him.

Walking up to the door, I pulled on a pair of leather gloves before I jimmied the lock, granting myself entrance. To my surprise, an alarm didn't go off as I expected. I thought all rich white people had alarm systems. *His alcoholic ass probably forgot to set it,* I thought, as I maneuvered my way through the house in the dark. I made my way up the round staircase, pulling my gun out as I reached the bedroom where I found the old drunk sleeping.

Thanks to the silencer that was securely screwed on my gun, I sent a silent bullet right in his ass that woke him out of his peaceful slumber.

"ARGUHH!" he screamed out like a little bitch.

"Wake yo' ass up, bitch," I smiled sinisterly.

He jumped up as if he didn't know where he was or what was going on. I found this shit to be quite comical.

"What…what—"

"I'm doing all the fucking talking around here," I said before slapping him in the face with my gun. "Now, get out of the bed and walk downstairs," I instructed, with my gun aimed right at his head.

He looked as if he wanted to protest, so I let out a shot that barely missed his ear to let him know that I wasn't playing with his pale faced ass. It may have been dark as fuck in the house, but I had been shooting long enough to know when I was going to miss my target or not. He was probably going to have a little flesh wound on his ear, but nothing serious.

Finally catching the hint, he got out of the bed as best as he could, considering the wound he had in his ass. I slowly followed behind him as he led the way to the downstairs area.

"Where—"

WHAP!

"Didn't I tell yo' ass not to say shit. Hardheaded muthafucka, take yo' ass to the fucking kitchen," I instructed, getting annoyed with his lack of comprehension skills.

He limped his ass to the kitchen, dropping little droplets of blood behind him, and I tried to contain my laughter as I walked behind him. This shit was so pitiful to me. I never thought I would have so much fun killing somebody before, but this shit was about to take the cake.

I pulled out one of the fancy ass chairs from the table he had in there and nodded my head at it for him to sit down in it. I knew the fucker was going to have a hard time doing so with a hole in his ass cheek, but I really didn't give a fuck. That shit was minor compared to what I had in store for him. When he sat down, I hit the light switch on and stood in front of him.

"You remember me?" I questioned.

He stared at me with squinted eyes for a few before his eyes bucked with recognition.

"You...you're him," he said.

I smiled to myself as I opened all his drawers until I came

across the one with the knives in it. I reached in a pulled out the sharpest one. Out the corner of my eye, I could see him trying to get out of the chair and run, but he didn't make it far after a bullet tore through his knee.

"AHHH, FUCK!"

"You gotta be quicker than that, old man," I said, while walking over to where he was lying on the floor, with the knife in my hand.

I pulled him up by the collar of his pajama shirt and shoved him back in the chair. Before he could even say or do anything else, I took the knife and lodged it right in his throat where his Adam's apple was. I didn't even bat an eye at all the blood that came gushing out. I pulled it out and stabbed him right in his heart.

Somewhere, I snapped, and just continued to stab his ass before I knew it. By the time I snapped back into reality, I probably had stabbed him over 100 times. I looked down at him in satisfaction that his face was unrecognizable. With a smile on my face, I walked out of his house just as swiftly as I had walked in.

One down, three to go.

Eleven – Lady

I looked around the club in amazement. I couldn't believe that the vision that I had for my twenty-third birthday had come together so well, thanks to everyone that worked at my business K&L Events, and the goon squad. They all had put in countless hours of work on such short notice to help make sure I had a birthday to remember. This was the first birthday I was celebrating in two years, and the first birthday I was celebrating with Lace period. So, it was kind of bittersweet for me.

All day, Lace and I had begun running around together to get ready for tonight, and here we were walking in together. Since Lace was so damn antisocial, getting him to show up was like pulling teeth. I had to beg and plead with him to be a part of it because he hates being around a lot of people, big crowds, and people he doesn't know. Once I finally got him to give in, I had no more problems out of him.

"Hello, Miss Lady," I heard from behind me.

"Oh my gosh!" I yelled out in shock as I made my way to a familiar face.

It had been over two years since the late time I saw Candace. The last time we had spoken was when I was in the hospital when

Ry and them saved me from Omar, and I had just found out I was pregnant. From what I heard last, she had moved out of Virginia.

"Happy birthday, chick," she smiled.

"Thank you, Candace. Wow, you look so good," I gushed.

I wasn't lying, either. Candace used to be a little on the slimmer side, but now she was thick in all the right places. It didn't look as if she had an ounce of fat on her except for her ass, but it looked good on her.

"Me? You look beautiful! You are working that dress," she said.

"Thank you. Oh my gosh, come on, we have a lot of catching up to do," I said as I took her hand.

When I turned around, I noticed that Lace was no longer behind me. I looked around to see if I spotted him in the crowd anywhere, but I couldn't, so I just shrugged it off. *He'll pop up eventually*, I thought, as Candace and I made our way to the VIP section. When we got there, of course the goon squad had bottles popped and was turning up without me.

"Y'all just couldn't wait for me, huh?" I yelled over the music.

"Yo, happy birthday, Lady!" they all yelled simultaneously.

They all made their way over to me and pulled me into hugs, but I noticed Ry stopped dead in his tracks and didn't bother to come closer when he saw Candace by my side. I had absolutely forgotten about the issues between the two of them regarding the death of her ex-boyfriend, and was feeling bad about the awkward position I had just put both of them in.

"Candace, I am so sorry. I forgot..."

I trailed my sentence off when she shook her head and turned towards me. "It's fine, Lady. Honestly, I'm okay. It's your night and I wouldn't dare ruin it. I come in peace," she said.

I searched her eyes for any sign of doubt but couldn't find any. If she said she was okay, then I was going to take her word for it. The moment I got the slightest inkling that she was beginning to get uncomfortable being around Ry, then I was going to swoop her away for some girl time on the dance floor.

"Okay, boo, you got it. Come on so I can show you a picture of the twins," I said as I found us a seat.

"Twins? I didn't know you were pregnant with twins, Lady! I bet they're beautiful."

The whole time we walked away, I could feel Ry's eyes on us. It was like he wanted to say something, but his feet wouldn't move from the spot he was in. If I knew him like I did, eventually, he would find his way over to her.

-$-

"I need for everybody to make their way outside; I have a very special gift I want to give the birthday girl," Toine said into the mic.

I looked around confused because I didn't know that I was supposed to be getting any gifts. As a matter of fact, I had specifically requested that there be no gifts, but of course nobody ever listened to me.

"What is it?" I asked Ry as we made our way outside.

Once again, I was looking for Lace but his ass still was nowhere to be found. He hadn't popped up like I thought he would and I was starting to get a little worried.

"I honestly don't know. That nigga ain't tell us shit about a gift," Ry told me. "What the hell you looking for?"

"Have you seen Lace?" I asked a question of my own.

"Nah, that nigga ain't my concern," he said nonchalantly.

I just rolled my eyes at him. I don't even know what I asked him for. He was still salty from the first time the two of them met, weeks ago. You would think he would be over it by now, but no, he just had to be difficult.

"You know what, you don't—"

"Oh, shit," Ry said, cutting me off.

"What, what is it?"

I stood frozen in time when I saw what my actual gift was. I tried to will my body to move towards it but I couldn't move. It was as if my feet were planted right where I stood. I didn't know if I wanted to scream, cry, yell, or what. I was in complete doubt.

"Damn, you ain't gon' come give ya nigga some love?" he asked with a cocky smirk.

It was as if that was all I needed to hear before I took off towards him in the six-inch heels I was wearing. I couldn't believe that Sire was actually here, in the flesh. I had no idea that he was out of prison, let alone was supposed to be getting out. I jumped up and wrapped my legs around his waist, ignoring the fact that I had a little ass dress on, while holding him like I was scared to let him go.

With my face buried in his neck, I could hear him let out a small chuckle as he spun me around.

"Don't be showing my shit to the world," he said as he cupped my ass.

I didn't even pay attention to what he was saying because I was still basking in the fact that he was home and in my arms. I couldn't hold back my tears any longer so I broke down crying right into his neck.

"Come on, man, why you crying?" he asked softly.

"I'm happy you're home. I knew you would come back to me," I told him, finally looking up. "You cut your hair," I shrieked.

Now that I was getting a good look at him, I finally noticed that Sire was sporting a bald head. Even though I loved the waves and low-cut Caesar on him, I would be lying if I said this new look wasn't sexy as hell. It gave him a more sophisticated look.

"Yea, a nigga couldn't do too much with it in that bitch," he said.

"I like it." I rubbed my hand over it.

"Nigga, I should beat yo' ass," Ry yelled as he finally made his way over to us.

"Why you feel like that, baby brother?" Sire laughed.

"How the fuck you slip this past me?" Ry asked the same thing I was wondering.

Sire let out a breath and shook his head. "That's a long ass story that I'm definitely going to have to save for another day. The shit is so crazy that I can't even believe it myself," he said.

"On some real shit, I don't even care. A nigga just happy you home," Ry said before giving him some dap.

I really didn't want to let Sire go, but it was only right that I let the two have a brotherly moment. I stepped back and let Ry pull Sire into a hug. I smiled big as I watched the exchange between the two of them. I knew that no matter how much the two of them fought, you couldn't deny the fact that they loved each other.

Not long after, Monty and Toine found their way over, and the whole goon squad was once again reunited.

A Lady & Her Sire 4

Twelve – Monty

The bass from the speakers in the backyard bumped as Kevin Gates rapped about how much his diamonds really shined, while kids ran all over the place freely. For the first time in two years, our whole family was together again, so we had a reason to celebrate.

"Yo, Montana, where baby bear?" Sire asked in reference to Nylah.

He had the kiddie pool in full effect, as well as other various things for the kids to do, but she was the only kid that wasn't in attendance. I took a long pull off the blunt I was smoking and let it fill my lungs before I decided to speak.

I hadn't spoken to Cola since our last argument and I honestly didn't feel any way about it. Whenever I wanted to get my daughter, I had to go through her sister to pick her up from her sister's house, or she would drop her off at my mom's house. That was fine with me, because that kept me from wanting to curse her ass out every time I saw her.

"With her stupid ass mama," I finally answered.

Me saying that caused Sire to raise his eyebrow as he shifted in his seat to give me his full attention. "What the fuck happened to y'all? When I left you two were damn near in love, what I miss?" he questioned.

"Fuck Nicola, man, and that's on my daughter. She fucking unappreciative and I'm not putting up with that shit no more. She act like I'm not good enough for her because I'm a street nigga, so I told her she can kiss my ass on some real shit," I told him.

I never thought I would say this but, I honestly feel like my life would've been better off if she would've just stayed away. The only good thing about her coming back into my life was that I gained a beautiful daughter. Other than that, it's been nothing but bullshit. Everybody that's been there since the beginning of Cola's and my relationship, knows that I had been nothing but good to her dumb ass. At any giving time, I could've been out in these streets dogging her out and having her looking stupid with all the pussy that was being thrown at me, but that was never for me. Anybody who knew me, knew that I was all about her and only her.

So for her to act like she all of a sudden couldn't be with me over some shit she knew from the jump, I'm not gone lie, the shit hurt and had me looking at her funny. I felt like it was more to the shit but she just didn't want to tell me what it was; so therefore, it was fuck her from here on out.

"Man, I don't even know who y'all niggas are no more when it comes to you and Toine." Sire shook his head.

"What the fuck?" Toine said. "Fuck I do?"

"Both of y'all niggas on some stupid shit, especially you. Toine, you put in all that work to get Lala back just to lose her *again* and let another nigga slide up in your spot. Since when do we do shit like that? I remember a time when we would've put a bullet in any nigga's head our women thought they were going to move on with. You see how I made Lady's life a living hell when she *thought* she had a boyfriend, or whatever the fuck that nigga, Drill, thought he was to her. You better get rid of whoever that nigga is and get yo' family back, nigga."

"You can't go around killing everybody." Lady rolled her eyes as she placed a case of beer on the table.

"Says who?" Sire asked, slapping her ass as she walked away. "Anyway. As for you, Monty, you just have to give shit with you and Cola time. I don't even know why you two tripping when the both of you know you love each other."

"Love don't have shit to do with this one, Si," I told him.

"Would y'all listen to this nigga though? He spends two years locked up and come out on some philosophy shit. Who this nigga think he is?" Ry joked.

I couldn't help but to laugh at that one, because that was some real shit. I remember a point in time when Sire would be quick to say fuck bitches, now his ass was sitting up here giving relationship advice.

"Nah, on some real shit though, I was doing some thinking in there. Some real heavy thinking, and my eyes got opened to a lot of shit," he said as he glanced in Lady's direction.

You couldn't miss all the love he had for Lady when he looked at her. Their relationship had been tested ever since they got together, but somehow they managed to always get it together. That was some shit that I wanted, something I thought I had with Cola, but she just wouldn't cooperate with a nigga.

All I wanted and tried to do was love her, but she kept pushing me away.

-$-

Buzzz, Buzzz!

I let out a groan as I reached over on my night stand to grab my vibrating phone. It was two o'clock in the morning, and I had literally just closed my eyes 10 minutes ago. I lifted my finger to hit the ignore button when I realized it was Cola calling, but something inside of me was screaming for me to answer. Sighing, I went ahead and pressed the green button.

"What?"

"Bear?" she sniffled. "Bear, please don't hang up. I need you."

Immediately, I popped up in the bed. Just that quick, I was no longer sleepy.

"Fuck wrong with you?" I asked.

"I…I need you to come get me, Bear. I'm scared. Can you come get me, please?" she asked.

It had just dawned on me that she was whispering. I was just about to ask her why the hell she was whispering when she said something that had my blood boiling.

"He won't let me leave and I don't have my car. I'm so scared, Bear. Just please come get me. I promise I'll never ask for anything else," she whispered into the phone.

I heard a ruckus on her end before she yelled out that she would be out in a minute, so I'm guessing she was hiding out in the bathroom. I shook my head as I got out of the bed and made my way to my closet.

"Text me the address," I said through my teeth before hanging up.

Seconds later, my phone chimed with the address just as I was pulling some basketball shorts over my ass. I slid my feet into some all whites before throwing a hoodie over my head and grabbing my gun. If it wasn't one thing, it was certainly another behind my ditzy ass child's mother. But no matter how pissed I was at her, I just couldn't leave her out here like that.

Twenty minutes later, I pulled up to the address Cola had sent me. I didn't even bother using my manners to knock on the door. I used my gun and shot that bitch off the hinges when I heard her screams. I rushed to find the stairs and ran up them. I followed her screams to the bedroom where I found a half-dressed Cola being choked out on the bed by the same nigga whose ass I beat in the club.

"Get...get off of me!" she yelled as she tried to fight him off her.

Not even thinking twice, I pulled the trigger and put a bullet in the back of his head. Cola let out a scream when his dead body fell on her, until she realized it was me.

"Bring yo' simple ass on," I growled while taking my hoodie off and giving it to her so she could cover her naked body.

Cola rolled his dead body off of her and jumped up. I didn't even wait for her as I made my way out of the house just as quickly as I came in. I was irritated as fuck that I had to be woke from my slumber just to handle some stupid shit like this, because my dumb ass baby mama wanted to be on some hoe shit. *I should've just killed the nigga that night then all of this would've been avoided.*

"Thank you," her voice quivered.

I was so mad that I didn't even offer her any words. Anything that would've come out of my mouth at this moment would have been disrespectful as fuck, so I preferred not to say anything.

She cleared her throat before she began speaking again. "I wasn't there to sleep with him, if that's what you're thinking. It was only supposed to be one drink. I felt bad about the way things went down the last time he was at the club, and he invited me over for a drink. I accepted not thinking nothing of it. I got uncomfortable when I saw him take two lines of coke, then he started acting weird. That's when I called you," she poorly explained.

"Oh, so you called my thugged out ass to save the day, huh?" I spat.

"Bear—"

"Stop acting fucking simple out here, Nicola!" I raised my

voice. "You are not that fucking dumb. You know that anytime a nigga invites you back to his crib, he has plans on fucking, especially this late. Then you had the audacity to be disrespectful as hell and fuck off with the same nigga who got his ass beat in the club? What the fuck would I have told Nylah if he decided to kill yo' stupid ass all because you ain't wanna give him no pussy?" I yelled.

I was so pissed off that I was going well over the speed limit and didn't give a fuck. Only Cola had the power to get me like this. Had she been any other bitch, I would've straight up declined her call and rolled over to go back to sleep. No matter what I said or what was done, I always found myself trying to protect her from some shit.

Charmanie Saquea

Thirteen – Ry

I swaggered my way through the hotel lobby until I found the elevators and pushed the button to go up. I stuffed my hands deep in my pockets as I thought about what I was about to do. I was going out on a limb and wasn't sure if this was the right thing for me to do, but I was here now so there was no turning back.

When the bell for the elevator rung, breaking me out of my thoughts, I got on and pushed the silver button with the number six on it. The ride up seemed to go by quicker than it needed to and before I knew it, I was making my way down the hall to room 612.

Knock, Knock!

My heartbeat sped up with each second I waited, until someone answered the door. I could hear the lock to the room turn then came the door.

"Ryan?" she asked with shock evident in her face and voice.

Besides the night at the club, this was the first time that I had been face to face with Candace in two years. When I saw her at Lady's party, I couldn't believe that it was actually her. Things between us didn't quite end the way that I wanted them to, and I would be lying if I said that I didn't hold some type of feelings for her, even after everything that went down between us.

"I'm sorry," I said before turning to leave.

All of a sudden, I was feeling stupid for even showing up here. I had seen the text messages between her and Lady where she said that she was leaving tomorrow, but for some reason I just had to see her before she left. Now that I was here, I didn't even know what I was going to say to her. Even if I did, nothing would probably take away from the fact that she hates my guts for killing the love of her life.

"Ry, wait!" she called out before I could take another step. "You came all this way, you might as well come in," she said softly.

I turned around and looked at her as if I wasn't sure that was a good idea, but the reassuring smile she gave me wiped away any doubt I was having. She stepped to the side and opened the room door wider to grant me entrance. When I walked in the room, it smelled like strawberries, like she had just gotten out the shower or something.

I looked on the floor and noticed she had about two suitcases with her and they both looked to be packed and ready to go.

"You all set to go, huh?" I asked to make conversation so things wouldn't be so awkward.

She nodded her head before pushing a piece of her hair behind her ear. Yea, I'm out of here to tomorrow. I was just about to head out and get me something to eat though. You just caught me by surprise," she said.

As she stood on the other side of the room, I couldn't help but to let my eyes roam all over her body. It was pretty obvious that the time away from Richmond had been good to her *physically* if not anything else. When she left, Candace was slim thick, now she was just all around thick. The shit looked good as fuck on her.

"I can take you to go get something, if it's fine with you," I said, trying to get a feel of how she was feeling towards me.

"That's fine, let me just grab my purse," she said. "There's a bistro that's up the street that I've had my eye on since I've been back. We can go there."

"It's your world," I told her, letting her know that I was cool with whatever she wanted to do.

After she gathered her purse and whatever else she needed, we were on our way. We didn't say much on our short walk down the hallway, but that quickly changed when we got in the elevator.

"Ryan Lewis, wow. It's been a minute," she said as she looked up at me.

"Yea, it's been a good minute. I never thought I would see you again," I said honestly.

"I never thought I would be back in Richmond again," she said.

"What brought you back?" I asked as the elevator let us out in the lobby.

"Family affairs," she said. "Then, I heard about Lady's birthday bash and I knew there was no way I could leave without showing her some love."

"That's real. She was happy to see you though. It meant a lot to her that you were there," I spoke, as I started my truck up.

"Yea," she smiled. "So, how has life been treating you?" she asked as she shifted her body a little in her seat.

"Life is life. My daughter is growing every day and she keeps me on my toes. My brother is home now so that's one less thing for me to worry about."

It seemed as if since Sire had been home, all the stress I was under just suddenly seemed to disappear. Our family was back together now, so everything was falling into place and we were a lot happier. Especially Lady. The move Sire made showing up at the party as one of her gifts, was a gangster ass move.

"That's good to hear," she said.

"What about you though? How you been since you left?" I inquired.

"Happy," she smiled brightly. "That's really all I can say is I've been happy."

"Who's the special guy?" I asked, as we pulled up to the bistro she was talking about.

I didn't know what I was feeling, but something ran through me just at the thought of her having a nigga at home where she lived now.

"What guy?" she asked as if she was confused.

"Most of the time when women say they've been happy, it has to do with a new relationship or some shit."

"Not always, Ry. Not every woman on a man for her happiness. My happiness comes from me. I moved out of this city and let go of everything that was hurting me or holding me back. I learned to forgive people and *that's* why I've been happy," she said, as she looked at me intently.

After that I couldn't say anything because she had completely shut my stupid ass down. I smiled a little because I picked up on what she was trying to say. Even knowing what she knew about me, there was no hard feelings on her part because she had forgiven me.

-S-

"Come on, girl," I said as I helped Candace get into her room.

What was supposed to be us going to catch a bite turned into us getting something to eat plus drinks; lots of drinks. She wasn't falling on her ass drunk or anything like that, but she was definitely feeling nice.

"Oh my gosh, Ry! This is exactly what I needed," she said as she plopped down on her bed.

I just shook my head and let out a little laugh at her as I made my way to the bathroom. I was going to relieve myself then get out of here so she could catch some sleep. She had already told me out her mouth that she had an early flight to catch, so now I was feeling a little bad about letting her have all those drinks.

When I came out of the bathroom, all of the lights were out except for the one on the night stand. I looked around in confusion, especially when I found Candace standing there in nothing but a lace bra and thong.

"Candace—"

"Shh." She cut me off as she walked over to me and put her finger up to my lip.

She went for my belt buckle, but I grabbed her hand to stop her. Since she was shorter than me, I had to look down into her glossy eyes that I could barely see in the dimly lit room.

"Nah, you're drunk and as bad I want to fuck you, I'm not about to take advantage of you," I told her.

"I'm not drunk, Ryan. Besides, who said I wasn't trying to take advantage of you?" she questioned.

"Candy, I'm telling yo' little ass this is *not* what you want."

"Let me make that decision," she said as she went back to my belt.

The voice in my head was screaming for me to stop her but I couldn't. She claimed she knew what she was doing so I was stuck. Plus, the shit felt as much right as it did wrong. Once she got my belt and pants undone, I let them fall to the floor before kicking my shoes off and stepping out of them. Candace reached into my boxers and grabbed my dick that turned rock instantly at her touch.

Her eyes never left mine as she softly stroked my dick, moving her soft hand up and down my shaft. I pulled my boxers all the way down and kicked them off as well, before instructing her to lay down on the bed. Without having to be told twice, she turned around and made her way to the bed. I bit my lip at the way her juicy ass was swallowing the black thong she was wearing.

As if she could feel my eyes on her, she pulled the thong all the way down, making sure she bent over giving me a perfect view. She climbed in the bed on her knees before hiking her ass up, waiting on me.

A woman that likes to take charge, I like that shit, I thought, as I walked up and slapped her on the ass. Ripples of waves moved throughout her ass before I stuck my finger in her pussy. As if somebody turned the faucet on or something, her shit was dripping wet. I grabbed her by the back of her neck, replacing my finger with my hard dick.

"Uhh, oh shit," she moaned out as I slid in her.

"Where the fuck you going?" I asked as I pulled her back towards me. "You wanted this shit so take it."

While I was talking shit, I had to take a minute my damn self to get myself together. The way that she was feeling on my dick was some shit I had never felt. I felt like I was about to bust already and all I did was slide in; I hadn't even stroked the pussy yet. After getting my shit together, I hit her with deep strokes as I watched her ass bounce back on my pelvic.

"Shit…"

"Ooh, Ry, fuck me."

Obliging her request, I grabbed ahold to her waist and fucked her like it was going out of style. I had been imagining what it would be like to fuck her since I first laid eyes on her in Lady's apartment way back. but this shit was better than I ever could imagine.

"Damn, girl," I said when she started to throw that fat ass back on me.

"Yesssss, Ry, right there!" she yelled out.

"Right where? Right here?" I asked as I hit her with hard strokes.

"Yes, ohh shit! Fuck!" she yelled while grabbing at shit that wasn't there.

I felt her juices raining down my dick and smiled to myself. That's one. She had just bust one of many nuts she was going to have fucking around with me tonight.

***

I turned over the next morning and had to remember where the fuck I was. I looked around the room and memories of last night flooded my head when I saw the clothes thrown all across the room. I looked to my left and smiled at the soft body that was lying next to me.

"You missed your flight," I told her as she stared up at me.

"I know," she smiled.

Without saying another word, I laid back down, pulling her close to me. I didn't know what the hell this meant or where this shit was going, but I was going to go with the flow. I know it would probably take a lot of work considering who I was and what I did, but if Candace could put that shit behind her then I could too. *Who knows where this is headed?*

Fourteen – Sire

"You sure?" Ry asked me.

I kept my eyes trained on the diamond ring that was in front of me. *Was I sure?* Hell nah, but I knew I loved Lady so this what I was supposed to do, right? Lately, I had been thinking about taking shit with Lady to the next level, but I wasn't sure if I was cut out for all that marriage shit. A nigga could barely do the relationship thing without fucking up, so I don't know how I was trying to be someone's husband.

"Fuck no." I shook my head as I backed up from the counter.

"No?" the salesclerk asked as if he had never heard that before.

It wasn't the fact that I wasn't sure if I loved Lady or not, it was the marriage shit that I wasn't sure about. It sounded good when I was thinking about it, but now that I was actually trying to put the shit in motion, I wasn't too sure.

"Ol' confused ass nigga." Ry slapped me on the back of my head. "The fuck wrong with you?"

I just cut my eyes at him before turning to walk out of the jewelry store. Honestly, I didn't know what the hell was wrong with me.

"Aye, don't sell that ring. He'll be back," I heard Ry say behind me. "Matter of fact, put that shit in a vault somewhere back there. Don't even put it back on display," he ordered.

I just laughed without turning around, because he sounded so confident that I was going to come back for the ring.

"Hurry up, nigga, I need to go holla at ma and pops," I told Ry as I hit the lock on my truck.

"Why yo' simple ass ain't do that shit before you brought me here? Getting my hopes up and shit. I should really beat yo' ass," he spat.

I laughed because this nigga was acting like I was about to propose to him or something.

"It's better I get cold feet now instead of at the altar, right?"

Ry couldn't even answer me because he was too busy smiling at his phone like a teenage girl whose crush just texted her. I scrunched my face up before trying to grab his phone with my free hand so I could see who he was texting.

"Gone, man, damn," he said, as he slapped my hand away.

"Who that?" I asked, being nosey and not giving a fuck.

"My Candy girl, you nosey muthafucka."

"You a bitch." I shook my head.

"Says the nigga who just bitched out of buying his girl a ring," Ry threw back at me.

Even though it was far from being funny, I had to let out a laugh because the shit sounded horrible coming from his mouth. I knew I should've just left his ass at home because now, he was never going to let me live that shit down.

"Yea, well at least my girl didn't beat my ass and got me being a sucker for her ass."

"Fuck you, Si. Candace ain't beat my ass. I was letting her get her frustrations out. She did just find out I was the one who killed her boyfriend. What was I supposed to do?"

"Right," I said, half listening. "That's another thing though, how the hell y'all fucking around when you killed her nigga? That's some weird shit." I shook my head.

Don't get me wrong, no relationship is perfect, but to be fucking the very nigga who killed the nigga you was in love with was some next level, y'all going to hell shit. I just couldn't see the shit going down if I were in Candace's shoes.

Twenty minutes later, we were walking through our parents' door. It felt good as hell to walk through the door and instantly be hit with the smell of food being cooked. Shit like this is what I missed when I was locked up.

"Ma! Pops!" I yelled.

Moments later, my mom was walking around the corner with a spoonful of food in her mouth. Before I could say anything, she was stuffing the spoon in my mouth.

"Here, taste this," she said.

I took a minute to let the taste savor in my mouth before I chewed and swallowed it. After she was done with me, she walked back to the kitchen with Ry and I on her heels. When we got to the kitchen, she did the same to him. She stood there with her hands on her hip and her eyebrow raised, waiting for our approval.

"Let me get some more, I couldn't taste it," Ry said as he tried to get some more.

"Boy, gone," she popped his hand with laughter. "So…"

"You already know that shit hitting the spot," I told her.

She just smiled before turning around and going back to her cooking. "So what do I owe the pleasure? Who in trouble now?"

"Dang, we can't just come over here to chill with our parents? Why you always think every time we come over here, we come with problems?" Ry questioned.

My mom turned around and gave us a knowing look that caused all three of us to burst into laughter.

"Who is it this time?" she asked.

"Sire's dumb ass," Ry quickly answered.

I swung on him and hit him in the chest before he jumped up and ran to our mom like the little bitch that he was.

"Where's Pops? I need to talk to y'all about something," I said.

"Right here, what's wrong?" Big R asked as he walked in the kitchen.

"How did you know that mom was the one? You know, the one you wanted to spend the rest of your life with?" I inquired.

My pops' eyes bucked and my mom froze in place before she slowly turned around and looked at me with a shocked expression. I shifted in my seat with a smile on my face because this was the exact reaction I expected from them. There was a point in time where I didn't have a steady female and changed females just as much as I changed my drawers, so to hear me talking about marriage had to be weird.

"I need to sit down for this one," my mom said, as she turned her food down so it wouldn't burn before sitting at the breakfast nook.

"Honestly, I knew I was going to spend the rest of my life with Nisa when I first laid eyes on her. It was only when I approached her that it was confirmed." Both of my parents shared a laugh as if they were reminiscing on that day.

"What happened?" Ry asked.

"She shut my ass down before I could even open my mouth. She was a feisty little thing back then, mean as hell," he laughed. "The only thing I had done was walked up to her and she held her hand up to stop me from saying anything. She said to me that she knew who I was and what I was about, so if I was coming to step to her trying to spit some wack ass line to try to get her, I could take my black ass right back where I came from. If I wasn't going to step to her like a man and respect her, then I might as well turn around and find the next bitch to run game on."

For some reason, I could really see that conversation going down. My mom has always been a no nonsense type of person since I've known her.

"So…" she said slowly, while looking at me intently. "You're having thoughts about marrying Lady?" my mom inquired.

I locked my lips before answering. I knew if anybody could steer me in the right direction and help me get my thought process about the situation together, it would definitely be the two people that raised me.

"I been thinking about it, a lot actually. It's just, we been through so much since we've been together that I don't even know if I'm really ready for that big of a commitment, or if she'll even want to marry me," I told her honestly.

That was one of the main questions that was lingering in the back of my mind. If I did ask Lady to marry me, would she even say yes. I know I'm not the easiest nigga to deal with and I do a lot of off the wall shit at times. Even though I try to ignore it and act like I don't notice it, me getting locked up put a strain on our relationship.

No matter how much Lady said and acted like the fact that I hadn't talked to her the whole time I was in prison didn't bother, I know it did. We'd hardly had anytime to talk about the shit because she was always at work and trying to keep herself busy. I wasn't sure if she was doing that shit intentionally just to avoid me or what, but I peeped the shit.

"Kasire," my mom said, breaking through my thoughts. "Do you love Lady?" she questioned.

"Yea, of course," I answered without a doubt.

"Can you see yourself spending the rest of your life with her?"

Pulling on my beard, I put some thought into that question. I highly doubted that I would find somebody else like Lady and I couldn't fathom the thought of her being with somebody else. "I can," I finally answered.

"Then that's all that matters. Those insecurities that you're having, you can just push them right on out of your mind. No relationship is perfect; it's not supposed to be. As long and you two can stick together through the tough times just like you do the good, you two should be fine," she said.

"I cosign," my pops threw in.

Just like I knew it would, this little talk with my parents was everything that I needed. They really helped put things into perspective.

-$-

When I got home, I smelled weed in the air and the shit threw me off because I didn't see Lady's car in the driveway or garage, and the kids were at her mom's house. I headed down the hall and passed the den, when I had to do a double take. There chilling in the den, with his feet up on my coffee table, smoking, flipping through the channels on my TV, was some nigga that I had never seen before.

I know her ass didn't have another nigga in my shit while I was gone, I thought to myself as I stood there in awe.

"Fuck is you?" I spat.

The nigga acted like he couldn't hear me as he took another toke from his blunt before slowly turning his head towards me.

"Nah, who the fuck are you?" he had the nerve to ask like I was standing in *his* shit.

I had to step back and laugh because this was the funniest shit that had happened to me in a while. I didn't know who this nigga was, but I had to admit he was bold as fuck. I tried to keep calm, but shit like this irritated the hell out of my soul. Next thing I knew, I was reaching behind my back for my gun. When I walked up on him, I heard the sound of a gun cocking but the thing is, it wasn't my gun.

"You gotta be quicker than that, nigga," he smirked, as he aimed at me from the couch.

No lie, that shit had me stumped for a second, but I quickly recovered. Just as I was putting pressure on the trigger, I heard something from behind me.

"Kasire! What the hell are y'all doing?" Lady yelled.

"Who the fuck is this nigga in my house?" I yelled at her.

"That's my brother, fool!" she said as she came and stood in front of my gun. "Put the gun down," she said in an even tone.

Sucking my teeth, I contemplated shooting his ass anyway because I didn't like the fly shit he was doing. Instead, I put the safety back on and put it up. When I did, Lady turned around with her hands on her thick hips. Shrugging, this so called brother put the gun in his lap.

"You hang around some very peculiar people," he smirked.

"Lace, where the hell you been? I haven't seen you in days," Lady asked.

I just stood back to get a feel of this new situation I had to deal with. I knew Lady had told me some shit about her having a twin brother out here in the world, but I didn't know that she had actually connected with the nigga.

"Oh, I met this bitch at the party and we dipped out."

"You dipped out, huh? So you been laid up with a bitch for five days? You don't even know her, Lace. What if she would've killed your ass? I wouldn't have even known because I didn't even know you left the party," Lady stressed.

"Gangster girl, calm down. I just had to see what this Virginia pussy be like. I was curious if it was better than that Michigan pussy I've been fucking all my life," he smiled.

Lady just shook her head and mumbled something under her breath before walking out of the den. I looked her brother up and down once more before following behind her. She had stormed off so quick that I had to go looking for her. When I found her, she was in our bedroom getting undressed.

"That muthafucka been staying here?" I asked.

She paused and looked at me as if I had asked the dumbest question of the year.

"Yes, where else was he supposed to stay?"

"Around my kids?" I asked for clarity.

Lady sucked her teeth and went back to taking her work clothes off. Now, she was standing there in nothing but her bra and panties and I couldn't keep my eyes off her body. After having twins, her body was still the shit. She had a few stretch marks on her hips, but that shit didn't matter to me; she was still sexy as hell.

"I'm not about to do this with you. You act like he's just some nigga off the streets or a nigga I was fucking while you were locked up. Plus, the twins love him as well as KJ, so cut all that out, okay?" she said, as she tried to make her way to the bathroom.

"He is a nigga off the streets to me. I don't know him or what he about. That nigga pulled a fucking gun on me, Lady. I don't trust him so he gotta go."

Like a demon or some shit, Lady's head did a 180 before she turned her body in my direction.

"He's my brother so therefore, he's not going anywhere. That's it, I'm not going to say it again, and we're not having this conversation again," she said, before rushing off into the bathroom and slamming the door.

I stood there in shock, not really knowing how to feel. It felt like she was picking another nigga over me and I wasn't about to have that shit. I didn't give a fuck if he was her brother or not. This shit wasn't about to fly; I don't give two fucks what Lady got to say.

Charmanie Saquea

Fifteen – Lala

"This is so beautiful," I gushed, as I held up the necklace that Darius had just given me.

He came in the house from work and told me to get dressed. He didn't tell me where we were going or what he had planned. The only thing he said was to wear something sexy. Lately, the two of us hadn't been able to spend a lot of time together between all the new clients we've had coming into Tracy's firm, as well as the new hours Darius had from his job. With our conflicting schedules, we barcly saw each other so it was nice to finally be able to have some down time with him.

"I got you something to go with it," he said, as he placed a ring box on the table.

That's when I paused. I was hoping like hell he wasn't trying to say that he was asking me to marry him. Don't get me wrong. I love Darius, but I wasn't sure that our relationship was ready to go to that level yet. We had only been together for a year and even though I don't believe in putting a time limit on love, we still had a lot of growing and knowing each other to do. I wasn't trying to rush into anything too soon.

"Darius…I…" I stammered.

"What's wrong?" he asked as he sat up in his seat.

"Is that what I think it is?" I questioned, still eyeing the ring box that I hadn't bothered to reach for or open.

"What if it is?" he asked with a raised brow.

I shook my head as I finally looked up at him. "I don't think we're ready for that," I told him honestly.

I had never been the type to beat around the bush. If I had something to say, I was definitely going to say it. There was no point in faking the funk or acting like I was the least bit ready to be in another engagement when that wasn't the case.

Darius rubbed his hand down his beard before placing his elbows on the table. I could tell that's not what he wanted to hear, but I couldn't and wouldn't lead him on like that.

"Why not? I thought we were in love?"

I sighed a little in frustration because this is not how I wanted my night to end. Darius definitely wasn't understanding where I was coming from, and I could tell this conversation was about to go left.

"That has nothing to do with it, Darius," I told him.

"Then what is it? Help me understand because I'm confused."

"I just got out of an engagement two years ago where I felt like I was pressuring him to marry me. I don't want to rush into anything and it doesn't work out, just to have two failed engagements under my belt," I let him know.

He slowly nodded his head before speaking again. "So it's because of him?" he questioned.

"Huh?" I asked confused. "This doesn't have anything to do with Toine. I—"

"I'm not stupid, Alani," he cut me off. "I know that there's still feelings there and you can't convince me otherwise. I see the way he looks at you whenever he's around. He calls you all the time, even when it has nothing to do with the kids, and you always go running when he calls. So, don't sit up here and try to tell me that the reason you don't want to marry me doesn't have anything to do with *him*. He's always around, even when he shouldn't be," he spat.

I just sat there amazed because he was speaking with so much passion like he really had a problem with my relationship with my kids' father. The crazy thing is, he never discussed the way he felt with me prior to this. I was under the assumption that he had no problem with Toine, so it's funny how this had to happen for me to feel otherwise.

"Hold up. Toine has been in my life since before I even hit puberty or knew what the fuck a period was. He was my best friend before we even thought about becoming lovers, so the fact that we are no longer together right now is not going to change that. Yes, he's always around because he's very active in his kids' lives and whatever has to do with them, he's going to be there and I'm not going to stop him. The fact that you even feel threatened by him is crazy because if I wanted him, I would be with him."

I felt like I was getting out of my skin a little, but I had to set the record straight. He was sitting up here acting like I was supposed to kick Toine completely out of my life when that was never going to happen. Toine had been there since day one and no matter what we go through, he's always there. He was there for me at the lowest point of my life, when people weren't even sure I was going to live through the night, so what the hell do I look like turning my back on him when he needs me?

Darius didn't even bother to say anything. He just scoffed and raised up from the table, walking away. Having a minor ass disagreement with him over Toine was never in my plans, ever. He was just going to have to get used to the fact that Toine was always going to be a part of my life for the simple fact that we have two kids together. I also needed him to believe that I would never cross that line with Toine.

-$-

I was sitting in my den reading a book on my Kindle, when my phone started ringing. I saw that it was Toine calling me and even though it was just past midnight, I wasted no time answering. He had the kids for the weekend, so I was hoping that nothing was wrong.

"What's wrong?" I answered.

"Yo, La, on some real shit, if I ain't never needed you before, I need you right now," he said with worry in his voice.

Instantly, I sat up on the couch and threw my cover off of me. I didn't like the tone in his voice and it was making me nervous.

"What's wrong, Toine?" I asked, as I got up to go put some shoes on. I was already dressed in a shirt and some leggings, so I didn't have to get dressed.

"I just need you to meet me at the police station. I'll explain everything when we get there," he said before hanging up.

Police station? I thought as I slipped on my Fenty Puma slides and was out the door. I didn't even bother to tell Darius I was leaving because his attitude had been nasty ever since earlier. I don't know why but for some reason, my nerves were bad and I was hoping like hell that Toine hadn't gone out and done something stupid. Even though he chilled and stayed out of the way when he had his kids with him, you never know what could happen.

I broke all types of traffic laws making my way to the station, and made it there in about 15 minutes tops. When I got there, I rushed in the building where I saw AJ sitting in a chair holding a sleeping Antoinette, while Toine paced the floor with his hands stuffed in his pocket.

"What's wrong?" I asked as I made my way to him.

He paused and looked at me. "They found them," was all he said.

I was trying to read between the lines, but I really couldn't make out what he was trying to tell me.

"Who? They found who?" I questioned.

"Antonia and Andre," he answered.

"Found them like, they're alive, right?" I asked for clarity.

I wouldn't have been able to take it if Toine stood here and told me that my babies were gone. Even though I couldn't stand their trifling ass mama, Heaven, I loved those kids like I had birthed them myself.

Before Toine could answer, our conversation was interrupted by an officer.

"You can come back now," he told Toine.

Toine made a move to walk away, but suddenly stopped without looking back or turning around. He held his hand out for me to grab a hold on to. Without hesitation, I linked my hand with his and we walked away.

He led us to a room where another officer was sitting waiting on us. I could tell all this was making Antoine uncomfortable because he couldn't stand the police, but he was doing what was necessary for his kids. I sat down in the chair next to him, silently, to hear what the officer had to say.

"Hello, I'm Officer Warren. I was on the one who brought the kids in. Your daughter, Antonia, was the one who gave us the number to contact you. She's a very bright little girl," he said.

I just smiled because that was so true. Antonia was very smart and sometimes too smart for her own good.

"Can I see them?" Toine asked anxiously.

"Oh, sure. I just wanted to share a few details with you, so I'll make it quick so you can get to your kids. Your son and daughter had to be transferred from DC where one of their officers found them in a run-down motel with no food. That place is well known for drugs and prostitution, so they do busts there regularly. Apparently, your children's mother had gotten caught up with some dude that was known for selling drugs in the area, and she was also wanted for fraud. Credit card fraud, actually. When the officers found your kids in the room, the officers had no idea that she had already been arrested five days before that, until the kids told us who their mother was. When she was arrested, she had never mentioned the fact that she had any kids. That's when they brought the kids here and we called you," he explained.

I was so at a loss for words about this whole thing. I could tell by the way that Antoine was gripping my hand that he was trying his hardest to keep calm and not go off. Never in a million years did I think Heaven would stoop to this level of trifling. To just uproot your kids and move to another state, hook up with a nigga you don't even know just to live a life of crime and neglect your kids, was some lowdown shit.

Her simple ass better be glad she was locked up because I would have beat the fuck out of her. Then, I'm more than sure Antoine would've ended her life. After he explained everything, the officer led us to another room where the kids were. It was a room full of toys and other things like that.

"Daddy!" Antonia screamed as soon as her eyes landed on her

dad. "I knew you would come for me," she said, as Toine picked her up and hugged her tightly.

"You damn right I did. Daddy's always going to come for you," he said, as he hugged her tightly.

Antonia's hair was all over her head and the clothes she was wearing looked as if she'd had them on for weeks. Andre rushed over to us and hugged me tightly, before making his way to his dad as well. Sad to say, he looked just as bad as his sister. His hair was nappy and looked as if it hadn't been cut since they'd left two years ago. His clothes were about two sizes too small. They just looked downright bad.

I could tell by the vein in his neck that Toine was two seconds from exploding, so I took my hand and rubbed his back to soothe him.

"Daddy, can we go home now?" Antonia asked.

"Yea, let's go, baby," he told her.

When we got back upfront, AJ was drinking some juice that I'm sure one of the officers gave him. I picked Antoinette up from his arms so he wouldn't have to carry her to the car. AJ and Andre shared a brotherly moment and hugged each other, before we made our way outside.

"Thank you," Toine told me.

I waved him off. "Don't do that. These are my babies just as much as they are yours. So, no thanks is needed," I told him.

"Lala, you coming home with us?" Antonia innocently asked.

Right then, it dawned on me that she nor her brother had any idea that I was no longer with their father anymore. They had already been long gone by the time Toine and I broke up. They didn't even know they had a little sister.

Toine stared at me intently as if he was waiting for me to answer her question. I felt stuck because there was no way I could tell her no but at the same time, I had a man at home that was waiting on me. All eyes were on me and I was feeling put on the spot. Sighing, I just nodded my head.

"Yea, I'll meet y'all at the house," I finally spoke.

Toine raised a brow as if he was shocked that I said yes. I ignored him, before kissing Andre and Antonia, assuring them that I would be at the house in a minute. Eager to see his siblings, AJ rode with his dad while I took a sleeping Antoinette with me.

Lord knows that Toine and I hadn't spent the night in the same house since the night before I blew up on him when I found out Alisha was pregnant. Suddenly, the conversation that I had with

Darius popped in my head and I was starting to feel a little guilty. I had basically proved his point when he said that anytime Toine calls, I go running. That had definitely been proven tonight, but it was more so about the kids than it was Toine.

I know that I had nothing to worry about because even though Toine liked to say slick little things, he would never try to cross that line with me. *Or would he?*

Charmanie Saquea

Sixteen – Lady

"Where are we going? Why I can't see? You trying to kill me?" I questioned.

Sire blew out a breath of air and I knew I was getting on his nerves. Ever since he came in the house with a nice dress, some shoes, and a blindfold, I had been on edge. He wouldn't tell me what was going on, where we were going, or anything. I thought it was cute until he put the blindfold over my eyes and told me I couldn't take it off until he told me to. Now, we had been driving for a long time and I was feeling like his ass was about to take me to a deserted location and kill me. His moods switched so quickly that you never knew what or *who* you're going to get with him.

"Will you just shut the hell up and enjoy the ride?" he asked.

"How the hell can I enjoy a ride I can't even see?" I questioned.

"Next time, I'm taping that fucking mouth, too. You ain't shut that bitch since we left the house."

I just pouted and crossed my arms over my chest. This nigga was so rude at times that I just wanted to slap him. How the hell he gonna get mad at me for having questions when he pulls random shit like this?

Not bothering to say anything else, I did as he told and shut my mouth for the rest of the ride. A few minutes later, I felt the car come to a stop and I got excited all over again. I heard his car door shut and I hurried to try to peek under the blindfold while he wasn't in the car.

"Caught yo' lil' sneaky ass," he said as he snatched the door open and popped my hand. "What the fuck I tell you," he said.

"Ouchh," I whined. "If we're here, why I can't see?" I asked.

Instead of answering me, he lifted me out of the car and placed my feet on the ground.

"Walk," was all he said.

"Walk where, fool? You know I can't see, you might be trying to make me walk into a ditch or something."

Huffing, Sire nudged my shoulder to get me to walk, so I moved forward and walked slowly.

"Step up," he instructed.

I followed his instructions as we went up a small set of stairs and stopped. I heard what sounded like keys before a door opened. Once again my excitement had returned as I tried to figure out what the hell was going on. Sire grabbed my hand and pulled me along with him as he walked. I used my free hand to see if I could

158

feel anything that would give me a hint, and Sire just laughed at me.

"Okay, take it off," he said.

I rushed to pull the blindfold off and a big smile came to my face. I was standing in the middle of a room with a lot of lit candles, rose petals, and a table in the middle of the floor. I looked around and noticed we were in a big ass house. I wasn't going to question him about it because I didn't want to ruin the moment.

"For me?" I asked.

"It was really for my other chick, but she canceled at the last minute so I decided to bring you," he said with a straight face before shrugging.

I swung on him but he moved out of the way before my fist could reach him. I went back to observing the room and my heart swooned.

"This is beautiful," I whispered.

"You like it?" he nervously asked as he rubbed the back of his neck.

"I love it," I told him.

He smiled before grabbing my hand and leading me to the table where he not only pulled my chair out, but he also pushed it back in for me. I gave him a questioning look as I tried to figure out what had gotten into him. I had never seen a polite side of Sire in the years that I had known him.

"Are you okay? Do you have a fever or something, because this ain't you?" I asked him.

"Hell nah, I ain't okay," he laughed, as he loosened his tie before sitting down.

I just smiled as I looked across the table at him with nothing but love. I had waited over two years to look this man in the face again, and it felt better than I ever could've imagined.

"I just can't believe this," I said.

"What? You don't think a nigga like me can pull this off?" he asked.

"Not that, silly. I can't believe I'm here right now. With you. I was so hurt when I heard that judge say 'life'. Then to have you turn around and straight tell me don't come back to the prison." I shook my head. "You'll never know the pain I felt."

Looking away from me and them looking down as if he was ashamed, Sire sat back in his chair. "I thought I was doing the right thing. I felt like I had messed up your life enough, then left you here with three kids… I didn't want to hold you back anymore. I wanted you to be free to do what you had to do for you. You just don't understand how happy I was when Ry came to see me and told me you were back in school. Every visit I would ask about you and he had nothing but good shit to tell me about you. I knew then that I had done the right thing because you were making something of yourself, without me," he explained.

"But it wasn't without you. You blessed me with three kids that gave me the push to do what I had to do. Without them, I probably wouldn't have been able to do it," I let him know.

Sire sat up in his chair before smiling a smile that almost made me cream. "I'm proud of you."

"Thank you," I smiled back.

"Now, let's eat," he said before getting up and disappearing.

I sat there, anxiously waiting, as he came back with two plates of food for us. Instead of something fancy like lobster or something, he came back with nothing but soul food that was bound to stick to my bones. I let out a little chuckle because I knew this was nobody's cooking but Mama Nisa's, but I didn't say anything. It was the thought that counts. I had never had anyone do something like this for me, so I was feeling like a kid on Christmas morning.

-§-

"I'm so full," I said, rubbing my stomach for emphasis.

We had just finished eating the meal that was prepared for us. All throughout dinner we shared laughs and memories of everything we've been through since the beginning of our very interesting relationship.

"When you gonna give me another one?" Sire asked out of the blue.

"Another what?" I asked, confused.

He didn't answer me, but I followed his eyes as they traveled to my stomach that I was still rubbing. When I caught on to what he was saying, I immediately shook my head.

"Oh no, I'm not having any more kids. I have the best of both worlds with Kasim and Kasmira, and we have KJ, so that should be enough for you," I told him.

"You'll change your mind after the wedding," he shrugged.

"I'm telling you now that…after the what?" I questioned when it dawned on me what he just said.

With a smirk on his face, Sire got up and walked over to where I was sitting. He pulled my chair out before kneeling on one knee and reaching in his pocket, coming out with a ring box. When he opened it, I damn near fell out of my chair. I was looking at the biggest diamond ring that I had ever seen in my life. It wasn't the ring that had me at a loss for words though, it was the fact that Kasire Armone Lewis was actually about to propose to me.

"Lady…bae, I know you probably don't believe me, but you mean a lot to a nigga. You're the bullet to my pistol, the weed to my cigarillo, the—"

"Really, Sire?" I laughed.

"What? You know I'm not good at this shit, so just go with the flow. Anyway, what I'm basically asking is can you see yourself putting up with a nigga for the rest of your life?" he asked.

Even though this was the hoodest and most thuggish proposal I had ever heard, I accepted it nonetheless. I mean, you can't really expect something romantic from a man who has been struggling with love for most of his life.

"Yes, yes, yes! I love you so much," I said.

"Yes?" he asked as if he couldn't believe it.

"Yes, boy. Now put my ring on."

Sire reached for my hand, but it was the wrong one.

"Wrong hand, Si," I giggled.

"Oh damn, my bad," he laughed.

When he finally slid the ring on my finger, I stared at it in amazement. You could just look at it and tell that Sire had spent some money on it. I still couldn't believe that I was getting married, to Sire at that.

"I can't wait to start planning the wedding. I can vision everything now, what's my limit?" I asked.

Sire looked at me as if I had offended him or something. "Limit? What that nigga Usher say? When you roll with a nigga like me, there's no limit. This is all you, baby. Do what you need to do," he said with a straight face.

I got up with a smile that I couldn't wipe from my face, and wrapped my arms around his waist while standing on my tippy toes. Even with heels on, Sire was damn near a foot taller than me.

"I love you, Kasire."

"Word?" he asked.

"Yup."

"I love yo' lil ugly ass, too, Lady," he smiled.

I let out a laugh before laying my head on his chest, listening to his heartbeat. Everything was finally going right in our lives. I was on a natural high because of the man I loved, and nothing or no one was going to mess that up for me.

Seventeen – Cola

"Here's your drink," I said with a small smile.

For some reason, tonight, I just wasn't feeling it. If I had to be honest with myself, I haven't been feeling it for quite a while now. Ever since that night where I was almost raped for a second time, my whole vibe was thrown off with this job. At first I loved it because it was the first time I was actually independent and didn't need anybody to take care of me, but now I just wasn't feeling it anymore.

My anxiety was back after two years, and it came back with a vengeance. Not only that, I was starting to realize how much time I was missing with Nylah. Before I took this job at this club, I had all the time in the world to spend with my daughter, but now it felt as if I barely saw her. On top of that, Bear and I were beefing something terrible.

Ever since we were teenagers, I would do something here or there to make him mad at me, but it was never to this magnitude. He was already mad at me from our little blow up at my house that one night, but this incident just escalated the shit. Before then, I could at least get him to answer my text messages, especially if they were concerning Nylah. Now he wouldn't even talk to me.

I couldn't lie and say that it didn't hurt because no matter what, I always looked at Monty as my best friend, so for him to just cut me off like this hurts deep. I know I'm partially to blame for the way that things are between us, but Monty never tries to understand where I'm coming from. Whenever I tell him I want him to leave the streets alone, he automatically goes off the deep end and blows up without hearing me out.

I only try to tell him that because Monty is really so much smarter than the streets, and I don't even think he realizes it. I want more for him than to be labeled just a thug because that's all society sees him as. Monty was so stuck on thinking that all he would ever be in life was a street nigga that you couldn't tell him shit, and that irritated the hell out of me.

I wanted him to want more out of life, not just for me, but for himself as well. Now, he didn't have just himself to worry about, he had Nylah in his life. I could've easily stayed in Texas and never even told Monty about Nylah, but I knew without a doubt that he would be a great father. I *wanted* Monty to be in her life, even though I knew there was a possibility that he wasn't her father. There was no other man that I trusted to love and care for Ny like Monty does.

"What's wrong, Co?" one of my coworkers asked. "I haven't seen that pretty smile since you been here. At least not a *real* one," she said as she rubbed a table down.

"I'm just not feeling too well," I told her.

"Well, why don't you call it a night? I'm sure Jimmy won't mind if you go home early," she said.

I nodded my head because that didn't sound like a bad idea. "I think I will."

"You should. I hope seeing that pretty little girl of yours makes you feel better."

"Thanks, love." I smiled for the first time since being here tonight.

I sighed as I made my way to my boss's office. I knew more than likely he wouldn't mind if I left early. Jimmy was a cool dude that I went to school with back in high school. He graduated two years before I did and always had the biggest crush on me. He did everything in his power to get me to be his girl, but I was so in love with Monty that I paid him no attention.

Tap, tap.

"Come in!" Jimmy yelled.

"Hey Jimmy, can I ask for a favor?" I asked as I walked in the office.

"My chocolate Cola bar," he smiled. "What's up?"

I just shook my head with a smile because Jimmy was always being extra. All these years later and his ass still wanted to flirt with me like we were in high school.

"I'm not feeling too hot, so I was wondering if I could go home a little early tonight?" I asked.

Jimmy looked up from whatever papers he was going over and sat back in his seat, looking up at me with those hazel green eyes of his.

"So your little boyfriend comes in here and causes a ruckus in my establishment, fucks it up and now you want to leave early?" he asked with a smile.

I rolled my eyes at him because I knew what he was trying to do. "I told you Monty is not my boyfriend and I had nothing to do with that."

"Shit, I can't tell, or maybe that nigga just didn't get the memo," he said, like he didn't believe me.

"Jimmy," I whined.

"Okay, okay, you can go. Feel better," he said.

"Thank you, I owe you," I told him.

"I'm going to hold you to that," he said.

I have no doubts about that, I thought as I walked out of his office. I wasted no time leaving the club and making my way to my car. I looked at the time on my phone and noticed I still had time to pick Nylah up from my sister's house without it being too late. The only thing I wanted to do was lie in bed and cuddle with my baby girl.

When I reached my car, I turned on my Jhene Aiko CD and cruised to my sister's house. Someway, somehow, I found myself lost in my thoughts and going in the opposite direction. When I looked up, I realized I was going in the direction of Monty's house. I don't know how the hell I got turned around or why I was going this way but for some reason, I just couldn't stop myself.

I had this yearning feeling to talk to him and see him since he had been ignoring me for some weeks now. Not only had he been ignoring me, but he had also been mistreating Nylah as well, and that was some shit that I just couldn't get with. I don't care how you feel about me or what you do to me, but don't mistreat my child. She's innocent in all this.

When I got to his house, I sat in his driveway for a few minutes, contemplating on if this was something I really should do. I knew how Monty's attitude could be and he had a habit of making you feel like shit when you were already at your lowest. Finally saying to hell with it, I got out of the car and walked up to his front door.

I knocked and waited patiently for him to answer. I knew he knew it was me at the door because he had a security system tighter than the White House in his house. I folded my arms over my chest just as the door cracked open.

"Fuck you doing here?" he asked.

I was trying to think straight, but this nigga was messing my head up. He was standing there with nothing but some grey sweatpants on that were hanging low on his waist, showing that deep v line he had. His six-pack was on full display and I just wanted to rub my hand over it.

"Can we talk?" I asked.

"Cola, get the fuck out of here."

"Bear, I..." My voice trailed off when I saw a pair of arms wrap around his waist and I was greeted with a devious smile.

"Come back to bed," some bitch said before she kissed his neck.

I just let out a little chuckle because once again, I had made a fool of myself when it comes to Monty. I'm starting to regret the

172

day I ever brought my ass back to Virginia. Nothing was going as planned for me, and Monty didn't give a damn about me.

I just rolled my eyes and made my way back to my car without saying another word. If Monty didn't want shit else to do with me, this was officially the straw that had broken the camel's back. I was done trying with him, I had nothing else to give him. Since he made it clear that he didn't give a fuck about me or my child, I was about to make some major changes for our better. *Fuck Montana.*

Charmanie Saquea

Eighteen – Ry

"When you coming back?" I asked as I scooted down in my seat.

"I'm trying to make it back this weekend," Candy said into the phone.

"I meant for good."

Ever since that crazy night at the hotel, Candace and I had kept in touch regularly. She had finally made her way back to North Carolina but we talked, texted, and Facetimed each other every day. We had yet to put a label on, or figured out what was going on with us, but we were going with the flow and letting things work out on their own.

I wasn't pressuring her into anything or rushing her, just in case she got a conscious about what we were doing later on down the line. So for now, I was enjoying the shit.

"I've been putting some thought into it, I even made a few steps to do it. I just have to find a house back home since I sold my old one," she said.

"How about this? You let me worry about all that. I'll find a house and shit for you so all you'll have to do is move," I said.

"Ummm, okay. I don't see a problem with that."

"Cool. Well I'm about to get into something real quick so I'll hit you up later, but I'll definitely get on that for you."

"Okay. Be safe, Ry," she said.

"I'll try," I said before hanging up.

As soon as I hung up, Tasha walked out the house with Ryley on her hip. I smiled when I saw my baby girl; she always brightened up my day.

"Why you acting like you don't wanna come in?" Tasha asked as she slid in my passenger's side.

"I was about to; I was on the phone," I told her as I took Ryley from her.

"Oh, it was that deep that you didn't want me to hear the conversation?" she inquired with a raised brow.

I just laughed because our relationship has come a long way. I could literally sit and talk to Tasha about anything now, but back when we were together, that shit was dead. Now, I'm starting to wonder if we didn't work out, because we were better off friends and ignored all the signs that were telling us such.

"Nah, it was just Candy," I told her.

"The one who…" She didn't say the whole thing, but I knew what she was talking about.

"Yup."

"Oooh," she squealed as she shifted in her seat to look at me. "Tell me more, how is that working out for you? Like, what's going on between y'all? I haven't heard you speak her name in years," she said.

Tasha just couldn't wait for me to "spill the tea" as she would say. I had given her a brief little rundown on my situation with Candy, but she didn't know the specifics. Even though we were cool now, I didn't want to make things awkward for her by telling her too much stuff when it comes to me and another woman, so I limit the things I tell her.

"Why you so nosey, dude?"

"Ry, outside of our daughter, my life is boring. You shut down the thought of me even having a boyfriend every time I bring it up, so I live through you when it comes to these things," she said.

Tasha was right about that; I did shut down that boyfriend shit every time she brought it up. It wasn't because I wanted her or anything. It was because I didn't trust no nigga that wasn't me, or my brothers around my daughter. Too much fucked up shit was going on in the world when it came to kids and their parents' significant others, and I'll be damned if I let something happen to my baby girl.

I would happily do the time for my daughter. That's why I didn't understand the shit that be going through Toine's head. Ain't no way in hell would I let Lala have a new nigga if I was in his shoes. Everybody knows how much he loves that girl, so we were shocked when he told us she had a new nigga. *Couldn't be me.*

"Ain't much going on between us, we just chilling. Shortly after she found out what she found out, she moved to North Carolina and that's where she at now," I told her.

"You gonna try to pursue a relationship with her?" she asked, giving Ryley some animal crackers she had in her hand.

"I wouldn't say all that, Tash. I don't know how to bounce back from that, so we taking it slow. You know, going day by day."

"That's good, but it sounds like it doesn't bother her anymore, Ry. Don't get me wrong, I'm pretty sure it's always going to be in the back of her head, but you two will never know how things can potentially go between you if you keep avoiding the subject. Obviously she sees something in you that has her willing to put that behind her. You need to talk to her and figure it out. Communication is key," Tasha said.

Once again, my daughter's mother was making some valid points. This was why I was happy I decided to keep her ass around on some friend shit. She helped me out a lot, especially when Lady was too busy for me to talk to these days. She wasn't afraid to say what I needed to hear instead of what I wanted to hear. I couldn't have picked a better mother for Ryley.

"You right," I said.

"I know. Now come in so you can fix something for me," she said as she got out of the car.

"That's gonna cost you, I'm not no handyman."

Tasha stopped walking and looked at me like I was crazy. "Nine and a half months of pregnancy, 16 hours of labor, 3 pushes, and 6 stitches is payment enough, nigga. Don't do me."

"Why she so extra?" I asked Ryley before kissing one of her chubby cheeks.

I smiled when Ryley tried to put one of her wet ass animal crackers in my mouth. Looking at her had me thinking that I wouldn't mind having another kid sometime soon. This time, I wanted to be settled down and in a committed relationship with the mother before I brought another child into this world.

Nineteen – Sire

Today was my first day since I had been home, having my kids all day. I paid for Lady's mom to have a little spa day to herself since she had been a big help with them while Lady was at work, or whenever my mom didn't have them. Lady didn't think I was capable of handling all three of my kids without her, so I was sure as hell about to prove her ass wrong.

So far, I hadn't burnt the house down or anything yet, but I if I still had some hair, I probably would've pulled the shit out by now. I definitely had to take my hat off to Lady and all the single mothers of the world, because this shit was harder than it looked and I was only an hour into the game. There was no way in hell I could do this shit every day, especially with three kids that were all the same age.

"Aye, sit yo' bad ass down!" I yelled as I swooped KJ up in my arms.

This little nigga right here was a handful on his own. So far, he had already taken his pull-up off, which I think he was trying to tell me to kiss his ass and now he was running around the house naked. Just as I sat him down to put his pull-up back on, my phone started ringing. I reached in my pocket and pulled it out to see that

Lady was calling me.

"What yo' ass want?" I asked.

She giggled into the phone like something was funny, but I must have missed the joke. "How's daddy duty going?" she asked through her laughter.

"Wonderful, delightful, extravagant," I said through my teeth as I tried to put KJ's pull up on.

Just as she was saying something else, I heard a commotion coming from the kitchen that sounded like pots and pans falling. *Oh my God*, I thought. This was just what I needed, for Lady to hear some shit then get to panicking, thinking we was over here tearing the house up.

"What was that?" she asked, after being quiet for a few seconds.

"What was what?" I feigned dumb.

"Sire, did you put the gate up in the kitchen like I told you to?" she asked.

"What gate?"

This time, I really was lost. Lady had left here with so many instructions that I could hardly keep up. One thing I don't remember, though, was her saying shit about a damn gate that needed to be put up.

"Si," she sighed. "I told you to put the baby gate at the top of the stairs and the bottom of the stairs so the kids wouldn't go up the stairs of fall down them. Then, I told you to put one up in the walkway of the kitchen so they couldn't get in there. Your kids are some busybodies and get into everything if you don't keep a tight watch on them," she said.

"I see," I mumbled, as I got up to see what the twins had gotten into.

"You know what, I'm on my way home, I knew this was a bad idea," she said.

"Nah, man. Chill out, I got this. I'm they daddy, I can take care of them just as good as anybody else can," I said, starting to feel some type of way.

"I'm not saying you can't, Sire, but it's three to one over there and I'm pretty sure the kids are winning. I just don't want you to get overwhelmed. I have no doubts that you can take care of them," she said.

I couldn't even focus on what Lady was saying, because I was standing in the middle of the kitchen watching my bad ass twins playing around in some flour that I don't even know how they got ahold to. I knew without a doubt that Lady would kick my ass if she saw the shit I was seeing now. I was two seconds away from telling her to bring her ass home now, but I didn't want her thinking I couldn't handle this.

"Aye, stop by the store and buy some flour before you get home," I said and quickly hung up before she could say anything else. "Y'all mama gon' kill us." I shook my head.

I sighed and walked away to put KJ in his playpen, so I wouldn't have to worry about him while I gave the twins a bath.

"And to think, I asked your mama for another one," I said as I carried them to the bathroom.

Kasim had the nerve to laugh like he really knew what I was saying, while Kasmira paid me no mind. She was really her mother's child. She may have looked like me, but she acted like Lady all the way. One twin had my personality and the other had hers. Then, there was KJ who was me all the way. Every day I thanked God that KJ was more like me than he was Lexus. I was grateful that he didn't have any of her hoe ass traits because that wouldn't have been a good look for any child of mine.

I have no doubts that I made the right decision by letting Lady adopt KJ. He would never know he had a hoe for a birth mother if I had anything to do with it. As far as he or anyone else knows, Lady is his real mom and if anybody has something to say about it, they can come see me.

-§-

"There all down for the count," Lady said as she walked in our room.

I guess I was too playful for my kids because whenever I tried to get them to go to bed, they would look at me and laugh, thinking it was playtime, so I left that task to their mom. Lady had only been gone for a total of 10 minutes, and they were all sleep. I shook my head and zipped up my pants.

"No lie, my respect for you grew so much today. That was some difficult shit," I told her honestly.

"Yea," she sighed. "There's nothing easy about being a parent," she said as she laid on the bed on her stomach, watching me as I got dressed.

After laying low for a while, it was officially back to business for me tonight. We had a business transaction to do with our connect tonight, and I was officially showing my face after being gone for over two years. I figured I had sat around on my ass long enough, I couldn't let my girl be the only one bringing something to the table in this family. I was the man, so it was my job to provide. I would never tell her to stop working if that's what she really wanted to, especially since she has her own business. I was going to support her in whatever she wanted to do, but I wasn't going to sit on my ass and let her be the breadwinner either. She did that shit while I was locked up, but I'm home now.

"I'll be back," I said as I bent down and kissed her lips.

"I'll be waiting up."

I slapped her ass and watched it jiggled before walking out of the room. I pulled my phone from my pocket and sent the guys a text to let them know I was on my way.

Me: *Leaving the house now.*

I peeked into the kids' room and watched them sleep for a few seconds before I left the house. I noticed that my tank was a little low, so I was going to have to stop by the gas station after I swooped past Ry's house and picked him up. I was happy his little nappy headed ass lived in the same neighborhood.

I honked the horn as I pulled into his driveway. A few seconds later, this nigga came out dressed in all black like the grim reaper.

"Punk ass big brother," he greeted me as he got in my car.

"Pain in my ass," I greeted him back. "Check it, I gotta stop by the gas station before we meet up with these burrito eating muthafuckas," I told him.

"That's cool, I need to get me something to roll this weed with anyway."

With that, I headed to the gas station so we could fill up before we headed to this bullshit. On the way there, Ry and I made small talk. He was happy as hell when I told him that I finally popped the question and Lady said yes.

"Nigga! Why the hell you ain't do it in front of the family? You know that's some shit we wanted to see," he smiled.

"Nigga, I had to hurry up and do that shit before I lost my nerve. I didn't even know what hand to put the ring on or nothing. Lady had to tell me. That's some sad shit." I shook my head as I thought back to that night.

"Man, I can't believe this. My brother really about to be a married man," Ry laughed.

"What the hell is so funny?" I asked as we pulled into the gas station.

"I won't believe it until you say 'I do'. You so wishy washy you might change yo' mind," he said.

"Shut the hell up and pump," I said as I got out to head in.

188

"Get me a swisher, fool!" he yelled after me.

I waved him off as I headed into the gas station. "Let me get a swisher and 20 on pump…" I had to peek out the window to see what pump I was on. I did a double take when I saw Ry talking to a broad, but I paid it no mind. "Pump six," I said.

After paying, I headed back out to jump in the car while Ry pumped. When I got closer to my car, I stopped dead in my tracks when I saw exactly who my brother was talking to. I was standing there looking at a part of my past. The more I stood there, the more my blood started to boil. She looked up at me and the moment our eyes connected, I charged at her ass like a raging bull.

"The fuck you doing back here?" I spat as I pinned her up against my car by her throat.

She tried to talk, but the death grip I had on her throat was preventing that from happening.

"Come on, Si, damn," Ry said as he tried to get me off of her. "Sire! Let her go!" he yelled.

Finally letting her go, I stepped back and gave her an evil glare before getting in my car.

"Sire…Sire, please!" she yelled after me.

"If you know what's good for you, you'll get the fuck out of my city," I warned her before I got in my car.

I watched in my rearview mirror as she gave Ry a pleading look, as they exchanged a few more words. I started getting pissed off all over again when it looked like they exchanged numbers. Ry knew our history and what went down between us, so the fact that he was even fraternizing with her ass was beyond me.

He got back in the car after pumping the gas and shook his head at me.

"Before you say shit, you need to hear her ass out. You always going the fuck off without knowing what the hell going on. You ain't learned shit from the last time, huh?" he asked.

I knew he was speaking on the incident with Lady, but that was way different than this. Lady wasn't Atalia. They were two totally different women that were in my life at two different times. *Fuck her.* I just sucked my teeth and pulled out of the gas station. I wasn't hearing shit she had to say, so her and Ry could kiss my ass.

Forty minutes later, we were standing in the middle of Amilio's warehouse while his pretty boy ass smoked a cigar. I didn't too much care for his ass and he knew it, but he was the only connect we had right now, so I dealt with him off the strength of that. I wasn't about to let no nigga make me miss out on my money.

"Kasire, I guess it's nice to see you back. Even though I will miss seeing Lady's pretty ass around here," he smiled a devilish smile.

I just knew his ass was trying to be funny by mentioning Lady's name, but I could tell by the look on Ry's face that Amilio had just revealed some shit that he wasn't supposed to. I bit the inside of my cheek to keep from saying some slick shit.

"So," he continued. "Does that mean Lady will no longer be doing the transactions now that you're back? I really liked her, she was built for this shit."

"Bi—"

"Unfortunately, Lady will not be doing business with us anymore," Ry cut me off from saying some shit that was bound to have his meeting end with a shootout. "Sire's home now, so he's taking his rightful place back."

"What a pity. Be sure to give her a kiss for me," he licked his lips.

That was the final straw. Before he could blink, I had my gun aimed at his fucking head which caused his bitch, Juno, to aim his at me.

"Bitch, you got one more time to say some slick shit about my girl and I'm sending one to ya dome," I said with nothing but venom dripping from my voice.

"Tsk, tsk, Kasire, it's all good. You have to understand there was no ill intentions on my part. Juno, give the men their stuff so they can be on their way."

Juno just stood there like he was about to start foaming at the mouth, and I was daring his ass to bust a move. Two of us weren't going to make it out this bitch alive tonight if he did, and I could promise you their last names weren't going to be Lewis.

"Juno!" Amilio yelled. "Ahora!" he commanded in Spanish.

With my gun still aimed at Amilio, I watched as Ry went to follow behind Juno. I watched Amilio's pretty boy looking ass through the slits my eyes had formed, as I thought about the bullshit he had just hit me with. I was still trying to calm down from seeing Atalia's sheisty ass, and now I had to deal with some shit pertaining to Lady.

A few minutes later, Ry came back in letting me know that everything checked out and that we could be on our way. I didn't say a word as I finally lowered my gun and walked out, still facing Amilio. When we got outside, Ry tried to speak to me, but I stopped him before he could.

"Yo, if I were you I would stop while I was ahead because it's taking everything in me not to hit you dead in yo' shit right now," I told him.

Catching the hint, Ry didn't bother to say shit else to me. I swear I did about 80 all the way home to get back to Lady so I could put my foot up her ass about the shit she had been pulling. When I got home, I pulled into our underground garage and rushed to get to our room. I was happy as hell that her bitch ass brother was now staying with their mom, because I probably would've ended up killing his ass tonight.

"He's home, I'll call you later," she said before hanging up and trying to jump off the bed and run.

I'm guessing Ry must've called to give her the heads up, but the shit was too late. I charged her ass and pinned her down on the bed by her throat before she could go anywhere. I found myself choking a woman for the second time tonight.

"The fuck wrong with you? You think you some type of Griselda Blanco or some shit? Bitch, is you stupid?" I was so pissed off I had spit flying out of my mouth.

Crazy of me to think that I could buck at Lady without her backing back. Her crazy ass reached up and cocked me right in my chin. How her little ass did that, I don't know, but the shit threw

193

me all the way off.

"No, nigga, is you fucking stupid? Don't you ever in your fucking life put yo' fucking hands on me!" she yelled.

"Lady, you better calm yo' little hyper ass down before I fuck you up," I told her through clenched teeth.

"Let me tell you something," she said as she jumped up on the bed and jabbed her finger in my forehead. "Nigga, do you think I wanted to be out there risking my life knowing I had three kids who were at home waiting on me? Three kids who already had lost their father and could potentially lose their mother? HELL NO, STUPID! I did what I had to do for my family! Ry came to me and said your stupid ass connect was about to cut y'all off because of some dumb ass deal he made, and so I did what I did for y'all. I didn't enjoy that shit, but I did it to ensure that you had something to come home to, you dumb muthafucka!" she yelled.

I sighed and rubbed my temples as I tried to process what was coming out of her mouth. I wasn't sure if I was mad because she did it, or because I was the only one who didn't know.

"Lady, I—"

"Kiss my ass, Kasire," she said as she got off the bed and left the room.

A few seconds later, I heard the spare bedroom door slam and knew I was in some shit. I was already calculating the total in my head of how much money it was going to cost me to make up for this one. I could hear Ry's words from earlier in the back of my head. *You always going the fuck off without knowing what the hell going on.* Maybe there was something wrong with me. All I know was I was in some deep shit and had some major ass kissing to do.

Charmanie Saquea

Twenty – Toine

"And you ain't kill the nigga?" Sire asked like he was disappointed.

I had just finished explaining to Sire everything he missed regarding the whole situation with that nigga, Darius, copping some work from us, while the whole time he was lying to Lala about him being a good wholesome man and working a nine to five. A part of me felt bad and felt like I was lying to Lala as well, but the other part of me felt as if it wasn't my place to tell her.

"Nah, because I figured she gon' find out about that nigga eventually and when she do, it's gone be a wrap for his ass anyway," I shrugged.

"Man, fuck that shit, Toine. The moment he walked into that meeting with y'all and you realized who it was, you was supposed to put a bullet in his fucking skull. It's some shit that you just don't let slide. I'm still trying to get over the fact that you even sitting back allowing her to fuck this nigga, let alone let him around yo' kids," Sire shook his head.

"I—"

BANG, BANG, BANG!

My sentence was cut off by the sound of someone banging on my front door. I jumped up and immediately reached for my gun, as well did Sire. Nobody ever showed up to my shit, especially unannounced, so now that somebody was here and banging, I was assuming they wanted some hot lead in they ass.

When I got to the door and checked the peephole, I saw that it was an older white man on the other side. I moved my gun out of view before answering the door.

"Antoine Matthews?" he asked.

"Yea, who's asking?" I asked suspiciously.

"You've been served," he said before slapping something in my hand and walking away.

What the fuck? I thought before slamming the door and ripping the envelope open. When I read over the papers, my blood instantly began to boil.

"This stupid ass bitch!" I roared.

"What, nigga? What's wrong?" Sire asked with concern, as he looked at me like I had lost my mind.

"This bitch, Alisha, just had these muthafuckas serve me with some child support papers," I spat.

198

"Who?" Sire asked.

"Exactly, a fucking nobody," I fumed. "On my mama and grandma, I'mma kill this sorry ass bitch."

I just couldn't believe this bitch had actually stooped this low. Seven kids and had never been on child support for any of them until her stupid ass came along. One thing I wasn't and had never been was a fucking deadbeat ass father. Ever since my first child came into this world I had been on my shit without needing to be pressured into it. I did everything in this world for every single one of my kids, and had been doing for her son since before I knew for a fact he was even mine. So, the fact that she would even file for some child support like I wasn't shit was crazy as fuck to me.

I picked up my phone to dial Tracy. I was happy that I had a baby mama that was a lawyer and that could help in situations like this.

"Daddy, what's wrong?" I heard from behind me.

I turned around to find Antonia rubbing her eyes. I had forgotten just that quick that she was supposed to be taking a nap in one of the rooms I had down here. Ever since I picked her and her brother up from the police station, I had turned into a full-time dad. Antonia and Andre were staying with me full time now, but the help from Lala made my task as a new single father easier for me.

"I'm sorry, baby. Daddy didn't mean to wake you," I said.

"It's okay. Hey, Uncle Si," she smiled as she ran to him.

"What's up, knucklehead?" Sire asked as he picked her up into his lap.

I left the room to give those two a moment while I waited for Tracy to answer her phone. I was about to go the fuck off and I didn't want my daughter to hear what I was about to say.

"Hey, Toine. What's—"

"Yo, Tracy, I'm going to need your services because I'm about to kill me a bitch."

"What's wrong now, Antoine? And don't say that over the phone, you know better," she scolded me.

"My stupid ass baby mama just had me served with some child support papers like I'm some deadbeat ass nigga. That's what the fuck just happened. Like who the fuck does she think I am?"

"Wow, you must be talking about Alisha. How about you bring me the papers so I can look over them for you. There's no way you should be on child support when you're more than active in your children's lives, all twenty of them," she said.

I ignored that slick little jab she took at me and told her that I would be at her office in a minute. When I hung up, I walked back in the room to hear Antonia telling Sire about her new Barbie collection she had swindled me into buying her the other day. She didn't have any new toys at my house so her ass went into Toys R Us and made a killing. Andre, on the other hand, was simple. He just wanted a game system and a few games to go with it. But his sister, she had to have everything she laid her eyes on. *Just like a woman.*

"You good?" Sire asked.

"Hell nah, I'm about to roll by Tracy's office real quick to see what she can do about this." I shook my head, still in disbelief.

"Shit, good luck, nigga," he said as he got up to give me some dap.

"Antonia, go get your brother for me. We're about to go see Lala and Tracy," I told her.

"Yayyy!" she yelled as she took off running.

-$-

"Lala!" Antonia yelled when she saw Lala sitting at her desk.

Lala looked up from her computer with the biggest smile on her face before she got up from behind her desk and met Antonia halfway as she ran to her. The little pantsuit she was wearing was hugging every curve on her body just right.

"Hey, baby!" Lala gushed as she kissed Antonia's cheek before doing the same to Andre.

"Can I get one?" I asked with a mischievous smile.

Lala cut her eyes at me before returning her attention to the kids.

"Lala, can I come over and play with my baby sister?" Antonia asked.

"Well, sure you can. You have to ask your daddy first, though," Lala told her.

"Daddy, please?"

"Or, how about this one. How about Lala, AJ, and your baby sister come over our house?" I said, being slick.

Lala looked at me like she wanted to slap me and I hit her ass with a smile that was sure enough to wet her panties. Ever since that night she had spent the night at my house, I had been doing everything in my power to get her over and keep her over. Most of the time it worked because I had the kids doing all the asking when I knew she would never tell them no. They were just making my job easier than it should've been.

"I'mma pop you," Lala said through tight lips.

"What I do?" I said sounding like that little girl off the video. "What I did?"

"Bye, Antoine. Go see what Tracy is doing while I get my babies some cookies," she said before walking away with the kids.

"Must be jelly 'cause jam don't shake like that, baby!" I called out to her, getting some looks from some of the people that were in the office, but I didn't give a fuck.

When I headed for Tracy's office, she was standing there with her arms folded.

"What?" I asked.

"Will you leave that girl alone, she don't want you," she laughed.

"You sound crazy, that girl loves me," I told her. "All my baby mamas love me."

"Ewe, I don't even like you and if that was the case, why you getting put on child support?" she asked, smartly.

"That bitch is thirsty for the dick and I won't give it to her, that's why. I learned my lesson from dealing with Heaven, so I took a different approach with her crazy ass, but the shit still came back to bite me in the ass," I sighed.

I hadn't fucked Alisha since the caveman ages and never planned on doing so ever again, but her ass just couldn't catch the hint. This was the only reason why her ass why trying to put me on child support and everybody knew it. I had a handful of other baby mamas that could vouch that I'm very active in my kids' lives.

"When was the last time you seen your son?" Tracy asked as she read over the papers I handed her.

"She barely lets me see him. I swear I haven't seen little man in almost two months," I told her.

"Why didn't you tell me this, Toine? We could've been put a motion in to get some visitation rights in place. She can't keep him away from you."

"Honestly, T, I never thought she would pull no shit like this. Even with her keeping him away from me, I still do my part. I drop pampers, clothes, milk, all that shit off at her mom's house for my son," I explained.

"Did you keep any receipts for the stuff you bought?" she asked.

"Yea, they all at home."

"Good, we're going to fight this, so we're going to need all those receipts. Anything that you can think of that you bought for him, gather it all together and put it in a folder or something. I'm going to make sure you don't end up on child support," she assured me.

I sighed in relief. This was one of the main reasons I made sure I had a good relationship with my kids' mothers. I have their backs and they have mine in return. Whenever I got into some legal shit, I never hesitated to call Tracy up so she could help me, and she never had problems helping a nigga out. Whenever I had some problems with my kids or just needed somebody to be there for me, Lala was always there. Icsha was just cool as fuck all the way around, but I didn't bother her too much.

A nigga like me just had some cool ass baby mamas that I could depend on for whatever.

Charmanie Saquea

Twenty-One – Monty

"I'm sorry, but the number you dialed is no longer in service." I let out a grunt as I hung up the phone and tossed it across the room.

I had been trying to reach Cola for a week straight, but the shit was to no avail. Usually when I called it would go straight to voicemail, but now she went as far as to change her number on me. I don't know why I was feeling like *I* had fucked up when she was the one who was in the wrong.

"What the hell wrong with you?" Ry asked.

We had a little down time, so all the guys were in his basement chilling and playing the game.

"This shit with Cola starting to piss me off," I stressed.

"What now?" Sire asked before snatching a bag of barbecue chips out my lap.

"I ain't been fucking with Cola after that last stunt she pulled, like at all. I'm talking no text messages, phone calls, or none of that shit. So last week she pops up at my house in the middle of the night asking if we could talk." I shook my head as thoughts of that night came back to me.

"Okay…" Toine said like he didn't get the big deal.

"Well, that was the wrong time for her to be popping up because I was fucking off with this little hoe I had met. So this bitch must've heard Cola's voice or something because she came to the door with basically nothing on, telling me to come back to bed," I finished explaining.

Everyone let out whistles, shook their heads, or looked at me like I was crazy. I didn't see what the problem was because I hadn't done anything worse than them, especially Sire. That nigga takes the cake when it comes to doing some fucked up shit to women.

"Would you like me to do the honors or you taking this one?" Ry asked Sire.

"It's all yours. Go ahead and get your right hand man together," Sire told him.

Ry turned to me, "Nigga you fucked up," he said, while pointing an accusatory finger at me.

"How when she—"

"Hold up," he cut me off. "It don't matter what Cola did or what she said up until that point. You fucked up when you ain't put that bitch in her place because to Cola, that was saying you was picking another bitch over her. Women don't like that, especially wifey," he explained.

"We're not together though, Ry. Haven't been since before she left."

Smack!

"Shut the fuck up," Sire said after slapping me in the back of the head. "Talk less and listen more, you might actually learn something. Now, it don't matter if you and that girl ain't been together since Elvis was wearing blue suede shoes. You around here killing and beating muthafuckas up over her, you be sick as hell without her, ain't been with nobody since she left—nigga, you love that fucking girl! That's your fucking wife. The two of you are acting out on pure emotions because you're both still young as fuck and don't know how to control yourselves. Let something happen to Cola and yo' ass gon' be the first one making this city bleed. Stop acting like fucking kids, work this shit out, and go get your girl," he said.

"Yea, I hear you and everything, Si, but what about the fact that she said she won't be with me as long as I'm in the streets? I can't make somebody be with me if they don't want to."

"Allow me," Toine said. "Montana, on some real shit, everybody sitting in this room has gone through that phase. Cola is just young and scared. You just have to stop treating her like a fragile ass China doll and put your foot down. I'm not saying be mean, shake her up or nothing like that, but I mean use your authority. Be like, 'listen, this is what and what it's gone be until I've had enough. I promise you that I will never bring harm you or my daughter's way.' That's all you gotta do," he said.

I soaked up everything they were telling me and stored it in my mental. With me being the youngest, I always learned a lot from the other guys when it comes to things like this. They always gave advice and even as stubborn as I was, I was willing to listen.

-$-

I used my key to let myself in Cola's house and was expected to be greeted by my daughter but, instead, was greeted by silence. I thought that was kind of odd because her car was parked in the driveway, so she should've been here.

"Yo, Co!" I yelled as I jogged up the stairs.

I stopped by Nylah's room and it was spotless as usual. I never met a six-year-old who was such a neat freak. Next, I moved on to Cola's room. Even though it looked as it always did, something was still feeling a little off to me, so I made my way to her closet. That's when I noticed more than a handful of her clothes were missing.

"The fuck?" I asked myself out loud.

I pulled out my phone to dial her number but once again, I was met with the message that her number was no longer in service. Next, I called her sister up to see if she could help me figure out what the fuck was going on.

"Hey, Monty," her sister, Sierra, answered.

"What's up, Sierra. Aye, where yo' sister at?" I asked.

The line quiet before I heard some shuffling. "She didn't tell you?" Sierra asked.

"Fuck no, so go ahead and get to talking."

"Usually I stay out of my sister's business, but it's you and you need to know. I dropped Cola and Ny off at the airport like four days ago. She said she was going back to Texas until she figured out what she wanted to do because she didn't want to be here anymore," Sierra explained.

I had to calm myself down as I digested what the fuck Sierra was telling me. Not only did Cola just up and leave without saying shit, but she decided to take my daughter with her. I can admit that since Cola and I had been on the outs, I hadn't been being as active with Nylah as I was supposed to, and that was wrong on my part. The fact that she was even considering moving back to Texas had me feeling some type of way.

"Good looking, sis. I owe you."

"Hey, Monty. Another thing you need to know is that Cola might be back on her Xanax. I saw a pill bottle in her purse when I was dropping them off, but I didn't confront her on it. Whatever you do just please look after my sister. She's been through alot and I just want her to be happy, and she's happy when she's with you. No matter how much you two try to fight it, you bring out the best in each other," Sierra told me.

"I got her, Sierra. Don't trip," I said.

Before we ended our call, Sierra gave me the info on where I could find Cola because I was definitely taking a trip down to Texas. I had given what Sire and Toine said a lot of thought, and I was ready to get my family back.

Twenty-Two – Lady

"What's up, Lace?" I asked as I walked into my mother's house.

He had called me, telling me that he had something very important to talk to me about. Ever since Sire had been home, I hadn't been seeing much of Lace because he had been staying with my mom. For some reason, he and Sire couldn't get long for the life of them, so that left me stuck in the middle of the two.

That was the last thing I wanted was to have to choose between my brother and my now fiancé. Especially since my relationship with Lace was still fairly new. I could tell that Lace had been feeling some type of way towards me though. He had been very distant towards me and this was the first time I was actually hearing from him in weeks.

"I need a favor from you," he said.

I looked at Lace with a raised brow when I heard that. Ever since he had been down here I had been trying to help him out with stuff, but he would always decline. He claimed he would rather get up and do things himself than to have me help him out, so to hear he needs me now had my interest piqued.

"What you need?" I asked.

"I have a little situation and I need to borrow a few dollars."

"Lace, stop beating around the bush and tell me what you need," I said dryly.

Lace pulled at the little peach fuzz that he had growing under his chin before licking his dry lips.

"I need $500,000," he finally said.

I damn near choked on my spit when he said that. I don't know who the fuck Lace thought I was to be having that much money just lying around, but he certainly had me fucked up.

"That's half a million dollars, Lace! Where the hell do you think I'm going to get that type of money?" I yelled.

Lace turned his head and looked at me as if I was speaking a foreign language.

"That Birkin you carrying cost about, $150,000, right? That Bentley had to run you about $40,000, no? Them red bottoms gotta cost about $900. Them inches in yo' head? I know that ain't no cheap shit. That ring on your finger? Shit, that bitch was about a milli on its own. So you wearing the $500,000 I need," he said.

I folded my arms over my chest because he really had me fucked up now. What I had on and how much it cost was none of his damn business. I made my own fucking money, so I could spend it however the hell I wanted to.

"Check this shit out, Lace. As long as my three kids are taken care of, I can spend my money however the hell I want to and whatever the hell I want it on. Everything that you just named was bought for me. My man takes very good care of me, so I don't have to spend *my* money. So exactly what are you trying to get at?" I inquired.

"That's some shady ass bullshit. You would leave your brother hanging like that, but I bet you if that nigga you was fucking needed it, you wouldn't mind doing it. You'll bend over backwards for his ass but it's fuck me, huh?" Lace spat.

My mouth fell open in shock. I couldn't believe that he had the never to be standing here trying to guilt trip me. He was right and wrong at the same time though. He was right because, if Sire needed me, I would go to the end of the world to do whatever I had to do for him. At the same time, if Sire was in some shit, he wouldn't dare come to me to help him clean his shit up. He would be a man about his and handle it on his own.

I was a little tickled that Lace even had the audacity to be mad right now. He wouldn't even tell me what the hell he needed the money for but expected me to just jump right to it and hand the money over. Even if I did, the money technically wasn't mine to give him. Even though I had my own business, it was still new, and business wasn't booming like that for me to be making that type of money. The only person who had that type of money was Sire and I already knew he wasn't going to be with the shits.

"I'm not about to do this with you, okay? You need me, I don't need you," I said as I turned to make my exit.

I hated to have to do this, but Lace was going to have to learn some tough love. Ever since he got here, I had been taking it easy on him and doing things that I normally wouldn't do, all because he was my long lost brother. Now, I realized that I couldn't be naïve all the damn time. Lace wasn't about to just use me. *Fuck that.*

-$-

"Mama, juice?" KJ asked as he pointed to some juice.

Grocery shopping with kids was hard enough, but doing it with three of them was something I vowed to never do again. I decided to take the kids out with me so Sire could get some rest, but now I'm realizing that was a big mistake on my part. My kids were some busybodies and into everything.

"Sure, KJ. You can get some juice," I said as I put the juice in the cart.

"Mama, I want out," Kasim whined.

"No, you...I am so sorry," I said to the man who I had just run my cart into.

He slowly turned around and smiled a damn near toothless smile at me. He looked vaguely familiar and something about him didn't sit right with me, but I didn't want to be rude so I gave him a small smile back before trying to maneuver my cart around him.

"All yours?" he referred to the kids as he stuck his hand out to KJ.

"Yea," I said as I tried to walk away again.

I don't know why but for some reason, he was really making me uncomfortable.

"Sup, nigga?" KJ asked.

"Kasire, do you want me to pop you in that mouth?" I asked as I lifted my hand.

He cowered down in the cart and covered his mouth with his hand. I shook my head because Sire was really going to have to be hard on his oldest child. He was already off the chain at just two years old.

"Humph," the man smiled. "Kind of reminds me of my son. I

had to beat his ass every day," he said.

When he said that, I knew it was time to go. I didn't even bother to respond as I quickly walked down the aisle away from his crazy ass. I didn't have time to be dealing with no weird people today. I just wanted to get in, get out, and get back home.

"Mama, I want out!" Kasim yelled, throwing a fit to get out of the cart.

"Kasim, if I take you out, you better stay right by my side and I'm not playing with you," I told him.

He nodded his head like he understood me, so I took him out of the cart so he could walk. I grabbed his hand and started walking to head down the next aisle. As soon as I turned the corner, my bad ass son made a break for it and took off in the opposite direction.

"Dammit, Kasim!" I yelled.

I should've known better, I thought to myself as I panicked. I turned the cart around with my other two munchkins in it and chased after him.

"Kasim!" I yelled when I didn't see him.

I went down three different aisles and my heart dropped when I didn't see him. I saw a lady in one of the aisles and was praying to God that she had seen what direction my son went in.

"Excuse me, ma'am! Did you see a little boy about two years old, blue shirt, jean shorts, and white shoes on?" I asked.

"Oh yes, yes I did," she said and I sighed in relief. "He was with his grandpa," she said.

"Wh…what?" I questioned. "He…he doesn't have a grandpa," I said.

I knew she couldn't have been talking about Big R because he was nowhere around here. Instantly, I started to feel woozy at the thought that somebody had taken my son. This was a parent's worst nightmare and I was losing it.

"Oh my God, you mean…? Oh my God! I'm so sorry, I'm calling the police," she said as she took her phone out.

I reached in my bag and pulled my phone out as well. My hands were so shaky that I could barely hold it still.

"What's up, bae? You—"

"SIRE! SOMEBODY TOOK HIM! SOMEBODY GOT MY BABY!" I yelled into the phone.

"What the fuck you mean? Somebody got who?" he yelled back.

"Kasim. He wanted to get out the cart and I let him even

though I shouldn't have then he…he ran and some lady said she seen him with a man and…and…"

"Yo, I'm on my way," he said before hanging up.

I was so distraught that I didn't know what to do. I couldn't fathom the thought of never seeing my son again. I made my way to the front of the store to wait for Sire to get here. I knew like hell when he got here he was going to rip me a new asshole, and I deserved every bit of it. All of this was my fault. I should've known better than to let a wild ass two-year-old out of the cart.

Twenty minutes later, I was sitting on a chair with both Kasmira and KJ on my lap, surrounded by police officers, when Sire walked in with the rest of the goon squad in tow. I had already told the police everything I remembered, but they still wanted to badger me as if I had something to hide.

"Y'all done here?" he asked them. "I would like to talk to my wife," he said.

He didn't even give them time to answer as he pulled me up from the chair while Monty took Kasmira and Ry took KJ from my lap. I followed behind Sire until he led us to a spot where there were no police.

"Tell me everything that happened. From the moment you

walked in this bitch up until the moment when he got taken," he said.

Once again, I told the same story that I had told the officers. Only this time, I included the story about the man I had run into. I told Sire about how weird he was, how he looked, and everything he said. For some reason, this shit just wasn't adding up to me. It just didn't feel right.

"Yo, Si," Toine interrupted us. "They want y'all to come look at the tape. They think they got something," he said.

Sire nodded his head and led us to where they were watching the security tapes. They fast forwarded to the time when I walked into the store.

"That's the man I ran into," I whispered to Sire, as I pointed him out.

I noticed now that he had been watching me the whole time, but I never noticed it then because I was too busy with the kids and putting stuff in the cart. When I was talking to KJ and putting the juice in the cart, it looked like he walked in front of my cart on purpose.

Out of the corner of my eye, I watched as Sire tensed up and a vein poked out the side of his neck. Something had him perplexed.

What it was, I wasn't sure.

"Here's when he ran off," I said as we continued to watch it. "Oh my God, Si, that's him! He has Kasim!" I yelled, as I watched the man that I ran into swoop my son up and walk out of the store with him.

Kasire jumped up out of nowhere and stormed away. I wanted to follow after him, but I wanted to see what was going to happen next.

"The cameras in the parking lot don't work. We've been telling our boss to fix them for months now, but he hasn't gotten around to it," one of the employees said.

I shook my head at that before I sighed in defeat. I answered a few more questions before I was free to go. One of the officers gave me his card and assured me that he was going to do everything in his power to bring my son home safe. I knew without a shadow of a doubt that if Sire had anything to do with it, my son would be home before the police could do anything about it.

I rushed outside to find all the fellas leaned up against Sire's truck. He was pacing around like a mad bull and I wasn't sure if I really wanted to approach him or not.

"Si…" I said cautiously.

"I'm going to kill that nigga, once and for all. His dead beat ass has crossed the line for the last time," he spat.

"Who? Who are you talking about, Sire?" I asked confused.

"The man that took Kasim is Sire's father," Ry clarified.

"Don't call that nigga that shit," Sire's voice roared.

Now it was all starting to make sense now. He looked familiar because that was the same man that Sire had damn near beat to death at the gas station a long time ago. I didn't remember who he was because that was the first and last time I had ever seen him. Then, I didn't know that he was Sire's birth father. What the man said in the store sent a chill down my spine when he said he used to beat his son's ass every day.

Apparently he knew who I was, even though I had no idea who he was. He was waiting for the perfect opportunity to pull some shit and took the first chance he got when Kasim ran away from me. *Lord, please watch over my baby and allow him to come home to me safely.*

"Ry about to follow you and the kids home. We got some shit that we need to take care of, so don't get to tripping or panicking if I don't come home for a few days," Sire told me.

I wanted to object, but I knew better than to argue with Sire when it came to matters like this. He was about to turn into that Sire that I didn't like, the ruthless one that nobody could handle, so he knew it was best he stayed away for a while. Even though I hated what was about to happen, I understood where he was coming from.

I just nodded my head and took Kasmira from Monty to go to my car.

"Aye," he said as he grabbed my arm to stop me. "We good, I'm not mad at you. It's not your fault so don't get to thinking like that. That nigga been wanting to get at me for years and he figured this was the best way to do it. I love you though," he said.

"I love you, too," I let him know.

He gave me a kiss before kissing his daughter and son, and sending us on our way.

I knew the streets were about to get hectic and Sire wasn't going to stop until he had his son back home where he belonged.

Charmanie Saquea

Twenty-Three – Sire

The Patrón left a burning sensation as it worked its way through my body. It had been a total of three days since that bitch ass nigga had taken my son, and I hadn't slept a wink yet. I don't know who I fucked over in my past life for me to keep having to endure some bullshit from the same nigga. His ass had been a fucked up individual for as long as I could remember.

As if beating my ass senseless every day of my life for 11 years straight wasn't even for his punk ass, he thought he could come back and make my life, as an adult, a living hell. I hadn't seen this nigga since I beat his ass at the gas station, and before then, the last time I had seen him was when I was taken out of his home.

I don't know what his personal vendetta was against me or why he hated me so much, but I was done playing with his ass. I wasn't that same ass scared little boy that he remembered me as. Now I was a ruthless ass monster that he had part in creating. A merciless muthafucka that he really didn't want to see, but was going to have to before he burned in hell for all eternity.

I snapped out of my thoughts when my pops sat at the table next to me. I was so fucked up that I didn't even know he was here.

"I just left from checking on your wife. She won't admit it, but she's worried about you," he said.

A small smile crossed my face when he referred to Lady as my wife. We weren't officially married yet, but I loved the sound of that already. If I had things my way, we would've taken our asses down to the courthouse and been married the day after I asked her to marry me. The only reason why I was waiting was because I know how much women love planning these big ass weddings and shit.

"She knows I'm okay," I said before taking another chug of the liquor.

I didn't like the way I was feeling so, like always, I was drinking to numb myself.

"Are you?" Pops asked as he took the bottle of Patrón from me. "You need to go into this shit with a clear head, Si. All this drinking means nothing but one thing—you're letting Armond get to you. If he gets to you then he wins. We can't let that happen. Clear your head up, gear up, and bring my grandson home," he said before getting up and pouring the rest of the bottle down the sink.

He was right, though. Sitting here drinking myself into oblivion wasn't going to help me get my son back. I couldn't do shit for Kasim if I was drunk on my ass somewhere. I needed to get my shit together because Lady was counting on me to bring our son home, and I wasn't walking through those doors without him.

"Good looking, Pops," I said, running my hands over my head that needed to be shaved.

"You know," he said as he took his seat back at the table, "when I was locked up, I vowed that I would never pick up another gun. Funny how things don't always work out the way we want them too, huh?" he said.

I arched my brow at him because ever since he got home, he had literally been walking the straight and narrow. Now, here he was talking about getting his hands dirty again and I didn't know how to feel about that.

"What about Ma? You know she not gon' be too happy about this," I reminded him.

"You let me worry about her. I'm sure she'll have no objections to the shit when we have our grandson back home, tearing up shit," he smiled.

I couldn't help but to laugh. Everybody made it seem like our kids were horrible or something. To me, they weren't that bad, they just had too much energy. My heart filled with love and admiration as I looked at my pops. Ever since the day I came into his home, he had shown me nothing but love. He had loved me long before then but when they took me in, all that nephew shit flew out the window and I instantly became his son.

He loved me more than my sorry ass sperm donor ever could, and he gave me something to look up to. I remember when I used to rebel against his love and affection because I wasn't used to it. All I knew was hurt, anger, and abuse from a man, so him showing me love was very foreign to me. Instead of getting angry or shunning me, Big R continued to show me nothing but love until I finally gave in and accepted it.

-§-

After two days of asking around about Armond's sorry ass, we finally had a location on where he hung out. Apparently, he was staying in some rundown ass house on the Northside and was known around as the local crackhead. I wasn't surprised that's what he had succumbed to, because he had never been shit anyways.

I didn't give a fuck about all of that though. The only thing I was worried about was going in, getting my son, and killing this sorry son of a bitch so I could go on with my life.

"Alright, so what's the plan?" Ry asked.

All five of us, including our pops, were sitting in the car waiting on my word to make our move. I had already assured them that I didn't need all of them to roll with me for this one because this one was personal, but they refused to let me do this on my own. They had already let it be known that any problem I had was their problem as well.

"I really don't have one. I would say just go in and air this bitch out, but that's not gonna cut it this time. We might hit Kasim, so just follow my lead," I said before getting out of the car.

I heard Ry calling me back but I ignored him. I was on a mission and didn't have time to think of what we should do. My son had already been gone for three days now and that was way too long for me, especially since I know what this nigga Armond was capable of.

As I walked up to the door, I pulled out one of my twin desert eagles, took the safety off, and cocked it. I felt a presence behind me and looked out the corner of my eye, to see my pops and Ry right behind me following suit.

"Monty and Toine went around back," my pops let me know.

I nodded my head before kicking the flimsy ass door in. I went in with my gun pointed just in case I had to put one in his ass on sight. Monty came up from the back of the house and shook his

231

head to let me know that there was nobody back there, and Toine said the upstairs was clear as well.

I was about to feel defeated until I heard a noise coming from the basement. I nodded my head towards the basement door and told everyone to follow me. I slowly walked down the concrete stairs and as soon as I got to the bottom, I saw my two-year-old son lying on the ground in a fetal position.

I put my gun up and rushed to pick him up. I looked over his body to make sure Armond hadn't been stupid enough to put his hands on him.

"Hi, Daddy," Kasim said.

"Hey, little man," I said, as I fought to hold back the tears that were threatening to spill over.

It was something about being a dad that made me feel soft as hell. I had never been an emotional person like this, until the day my kids were born.

"I knew you would come for the little bastard eventually," we heard from a dark corner in the basement.

There he was, the scum of the earth, slowly walking out of the darkness looking worse than he did the last time I saw him. I wasn't sure if it was the ass whipping I had put on him or the years of drug use that had him missing some teeth, but he looked like the piece of shit that he was.

"It's your call, Si. Just say the word and he's done," Toine said with his gun aimed at Armond's head.

"Nah, this bitch is mine," I said as I handed Kasim over to his uncle.

"Ry, take him to the car. All the rest of you can go to the car as well and wait for us. We'll be up shortly," Big R ordered.

Everyone looked as if they hesitated to leave for a second, but they trusted Big R's word. They all knew there was no way in hell that I was walking out of this house and leaving Armond breathing. When they were all out of sight, my pops spoke again.

"He's all yours, Kasire. Do as you please," he said, as he stood there with his hands folded in front of him.

Armond laughed like somebody had told the joke of the year or something. I looked at him through squinted eyes because I wanted to know what was so funny.

"This little nigga ain't gon' do shit. If he was, he would've did it by now. This is the same little bastard whose ass I used to beat until he pissed and shitted on himself." He continued to laugh. "Never forget where you came from, boy."

I disarmed myself of all my guns and weapons I had brought for him, and handed them over to my pops. He was talking all this big boy shit, so I had something else in mind for his ass.

"See, Armond, that's where you're wrong. That scared little boy died years ago, thanks to the man who took me in and showed me how a father is supposed to love his son. Now, I'm a grown ass man that'll kill yo' ass with my bare hands," I smiled sinisterly.

"You can't—"

I didn't even let his sorry ass finished what he had to say before I hit him with a right hook. I had done all the talking I was going to do. I let him recover from the first punch, allowing him to get in his stance, before I hit him with a jab to his nose, breaking it on impact. I was having no mercy on his ass.

You would think after all those years of beating my ass he would be able to fight, but he was no match for me. The roles had reversed and I was taking out all my anger and aggression on him. He tried to throw a punch but he missed, and that's when I went in on his ass. He fell to the ground but that still didn't stop me from raining blows on him.

I wasn't just beating his ass for me. This was for the little boy who used to go to bed hungry for weeks at a time, the little boy who was locked in closets for five days straight, the little boy who

234

doesn't know how to love correctly because all he knew was abuse and ass whippings. This was also for my mom. The lady who walked out the door with a smile on her face, only to never return ever again.

When I finally snapped out of it, his face was beaten to the point of no recognition, and he was barely breathing. I reached for my gun and my pops handed it to me. I aimed it right at his head and let off three shots. When I was done, I just stood there staring at him. The man that had been a plague in my life for so many years was finally gone.

My pops pulled me into his arms and led me up the stairs. "How does it feel?" he asked.

"Good, damn good," I said.

I had always vowed that the next time I crossed paths with Armond that I was going to kill him, and I had finally succeeded. Now that he was gone, I could work on being a better me so I could be a better father and husband than he had ever been.

Charmanie Saquea

Twenty-Four – Ry

"How do you like it?"

Candy and I were standing in the middle of one of the houses I had found for her. It was bigger than the one she previously lived in, but I was sure she would like it.

"This is nice, Ry. I love it, but…" she turned towards me. "I'm going to have to work two jobs to have to pay for it," she said.

The conversation I previously had with Tasha came back to my mind when she told me I need to have a talk with Candace and figure out where this was going. My ass was up here finding houses for her and willing to get it for her, but I still didn't even know where we stood.

"Aye, we need to talk real quick," I said.

"About what?" she asked.

"Us. Like, I need to know where this is going, what we doing, and why you wanna fuck with a nigga all of a sudden," I told her.

I had never been the type to beat around the bush, so I just laid it all on the table so she knew I meant business. We were grown as hell, so there was no point in us beating around the bush.

"Well first off, nothing is all of a sudden, Ryan. All that time

237

we spent together years ago made me develop feelings for you. I never expected it just like I never expected for you to be Rafiq's murderer. By the time I found out the truth, I was already in too deep, but I didn't know how to tell you. I moved away and went through some counseling, sought some professional help, and I realized the heart wants what the heart wants. I know it's wrong and I shouldn't even be here with you. I have no doubts that Rafiq's family is going to hate me, but I'm grown and I make my own decisions. Yea, it's crazy, but I'm willing to see where this goes if you are," she said.

That was all I needed to hear. I honestly didn't give a fuck what his family had to say because what Candy and I had going on really didn't have shit to do with them. If they felt some type of way about it, they would end up just like Rafiq and his brother: dead. Just like she said, we were grown so we were capable of making our own decisions.

"I'm with it if you with it. You already know from day one I wanted yo' ass, but I left you alone out of respect for you," I let her know.

"And I appreciate that, but I'm here now so let's put the past in the past and worry about the present…maybe even a future. I'm not going to say it's going to be easy, but we have to at least try," she told me.

"Fasho. Now, about this house…" I said. "…I did my side of the deal so now you have to hold up your end," I reminded her.

"I already put in my 30-day notice," she informed me. "All I need to do is start packing which is going to be a task on its own," she sighed.

"No worries, I know some people who can handle that for you."

"Now, I have a question for you. What about your daughter's mother? How is she going to feel about all of this?" she asked like she was skeptical.

I let out a little laugh because she had nothing to worry about when it came to Tasha. Maybe if this was the old Tasha, yea, but this new and improved Tasha wasn't going to give her any problems.

"Tasha is cool with it. We have that type of bond where we talk about anything. She might be happier than I am. Don't worry about her, you don't have anything to worry about," I assured her.

"That's nice, can't wait to meet her," she smiled.

I smiled as well because I never thought I would be anything other than friends with Candace, and now here we were discussing her meeting Tasha and other things. This shit worked out mysteriously and I wasn't about to question it.

-$-

"I'm so nervous," Atalia said as she paced my living room.

You nervous? This nigga just might kill me, I thought, as I sat in my loveseat twiddling my thumbs. We were waiting for Sire to get here because I told him I had something I needed to talk to him about, only thing is, I never told him that Atalia would be here. The history between Sire and Atalia was some shit that could never be erased, no matter how hard he tried to do so. Before Lady, I had never seen my brother love someone the way he loved this girl.

"Where yo' little nappy headed ass at?" I heard him yell as my front door slammed.

"In here," I said as I eyed Atalia.

Her ass looked as if she was about to piss on herself. She was literally terrified of Sire and I wasn't going to sit here and act as if she didn't have a reason to be. Nor could I act like Sire's actions weren't justified this time.

"Nigga you…fuck outta here!" he spat. "I know you didn't call me over here for this bullshit!" his voice roared as he turned around to make his exit.

This time I didn't even bother to stop him like I usually would.

240

This was Atalia's fight, so she was going to have to do this on her own. I did my job by getting them in the same room at the same time, now it was her job to do the rest.

"Sire! Wait, Akil is out! He's coming after me." When she said that, that got him to stop in his tracks. "You said you would always protect me no matter what, Sire," she said softly.

I sat there just looking between the two of them because this shit was like watching a movie. The shit was so suspenseful that you didn't know what was going to happen next. Where the fuck is the popcorn when you need it?

"Yea, that was before I found out yo' ass couldn't be trusted," he said like he was truly hurt.

"I'm sorry, Si. I was young. What did you expect me to do? I—"

I damn near jumped out of my skin when Sire turned around and suddenly grew wings, as he flew over to where Atalia was standing at the other end of the room. He did that shit so fast that I blinked and almost missed it.

"Sire—"

"Shut the fuck up, Ryan!" he growled at me as he held Atalia's throat in his big ass hand. "What the fuck was you supposed to?

Have my fucking back! Be the rider yo' stupid ass claimed to be! That's what the fuck you was supposed to do!" he yelled in her face before letting her throat go.

"I'm sorry, Sire, I'm so sorry," she cried.

Sire looked down at her like he didn't know if he wanted to believe her or not.

"You gonna help her, Si?" I asked, adding my two cents.

"Why should I? Where was she when this nigga was setting me the fuck up? Oh, I forgot, playing both sides of the fucking fence," she snarled.

Atalia just stood there with her head down because she knew she couldn't say shit to that. She was wrong as hell and there was nothing she could say to make the situation better.

"Aye, Tali, how about you head home and I'll call you," I told her.

The way Sire was looking at her, he was about two seconds away from slapping the shit out of her. Sire really wasn't the type to hit a woman, but Atalia might have been a different case today, and I didn't want to witness that shit.

When she was gone, I let go of a breath I didn't even realize I was holding.

"So..." I said.

"So, my ass. Fuck you, Ry. You know you wrong for even calling me over here to deal with her shit anyways," he told me.

"Maybe I am, maybe I'm not," I shrugged. "My only question is, what are you going to do?"

Sire shook his head while running his hands over his bald ass head. "I can't do this shit, Ry. If I do, then I'll have to tell Lady and explain to her who the fuck Atalia, is and I'm not doing that shit," he said.

I couldn't argue with him on that one. He was definitely going to have to explain to Lady why he was doing something for his ex. Not just an ex, but his first fucking love. I knew whatever decision Sire made, he would figure out a way to make it work.

Charmanie Saquea

Twenty-Five – Cola

"Mommy, can I have some ice cream?" Nylah asked as we walked down the sidewalk.

"After you eat your dinner, yea," I told her as we walked up the porch to my grandma's house.

Before I could even open the door, I was hit with the aroma of whatever she was cooking. It smelled so good that I couldn't wait to get in this house and eat. As soon as I opened the door, Nylah took off running in the house.

"What I tell you about running in the house, Nylah?" I yelled after her.

I made my way into the kitchen, but something Nylah said made me stop in my tracks.

"Daddy!"

I stood there stuck because I knew there was no way in hell that Monty had brought his ass all the way down to Texas. After standing there for a few minutes, sure enough, Monty walked into the living room with Nylah in his arms and my grandma right behind them. I gave her a questioning look and she waved me off.

"Mommy, look, it's Daddy!" Nylah said with excitement.

I rolled my eyes on the sly when she wasn't looking and sucked my teeth. "I'll be back," I said as I made a move for the door.

"You can't run all your life, chile," my grandma called after me.

I didn't bother to respond as I made my way out of her house and back down the sidewalk I had just previously walked up. I needed to get away from Monty and to clear my head. Nylah could stay there and enjoy her time with her dad, but I wasn't fucking with Monty right now.

I was so lost in my thoughts that I didn't even realize somebody had come up behind me until it was too late.

"Why you run out like that?" Monty asked as he wrapped his arm around the front of my body and swooped me up.

I almost melted when I inhaled his scent and my back touched his chest, but I caught myself. "Let me go, Montana!"

Instead of doing as I said, he took it upon himself to bury his face into my neck and lightly rubbed with his nose.

"You smell so good," he said with his face still buried in my neck. "I missed you."

"Monty, stop!" I said through my teeth as I tried to push away

246

from him.

It was a hard task because he had me up in the air with my back pressed into his body, but I was determined to get away from him.

"Nope, not until you tell me you love me."

"I'm not playing with you, Montana! Put me down and let me go," I said, as I continued to fight him.

Finally, he put me down but hesitated to let me go. When he finally did, I tried to walk away again but he pulled me back.

"Nicola, I'm sorry, alright? I'm sorry for everything. For not being there when you were raped, I'm sorry that you had to raise Ny for four years by yourself. I'm sorry that I can't be the man you want me to be, but I'm a street nigga and what you see is what you get with me. You either gonna love me or be without me because that shit ain't changing no time soon. You know I would die before I let anything happen to you or Ny, so I need you to trust me," he said.

I hated that he spoke with so much sincerity and that his eyes told me no lies. I wanted to be mad at Monty, but I knew I had no real reason to.

"You with me or what?" he asked.

I opened my mouth to say something but nothing came out. I was stuck. The only thing I could do was push past him and head back towards the house. *Was I ready to go back down that road with Monty?*

-$-

Later that night, I sat on my grandma's porch with my phone in my hand, contemplating on if I should call Monty or not. After I left him standing on the sidewalk, he didn't bother to come back to the house, and I had to hear Ny throw a fit for the rest of the night, as well as my grandma fuss about how I was going to run that boy away for good if I didn't get it together.

As soon as I worked up the nerve to call him, a car pulled into my grandma's driveway and out stepped Monty. I tried to ignore how my heart rate sped up when my eyes landed on him, but I couldn't. This boy had been doing something to me ever since I was 14 years old. I didn't even give him time to walk up the stairs before I took off for him.

"I'm with you!" I told him as I jumped in his arms. "I'm with you."

"Oh, I know. I had no doubts that you are. I was just giving you some time to get yo' head right. You crazy as hell if you thought I was going back to Richmond without y'all."

"I'm sorry, too," I told him as I laid my head on his chest while he carried us up the stairs to the porch. "I made a lot of stupid decisions that had something to do with us getting to this point. It wasn't all you. I never should've made you feel like you weren't good enough for me because that was never the case. I just wanted more for you," I explained to him.

He nodded his head as he sat down with me on his lap. I laid my head on his chest and wrapped my arms around him.

"You back to taking those pills?" he asked.

I tensed up a little because I didn't know how he knew that. I had just recently started back taking the Xanax because I felt my anxiety and depression coming back, and that was the only thing that could help me at the time.

"Yea, but—"

"But nothing, Cola. Just like you want more and better for me, I want the same for you. Taking those pills ain't doing shit but enabling you to them, then next thing you know, you gonna be dependent on them. That's how people turn into crackheads and I don't want that shit for you. Another thing, you not going back to that club to work. You went to school to be a physical therapist, not a fucking bottle girl," he said.

"I hear you, Bear," I said. "We'll get it worked out," I told him.

For the first time in a while, I was finally at peace again. The only time I felt like this was whenever I was in his arms. I was crazy to ever think I could get rid of him. I had never loved somebody the way I love Monty, and I could never see myself loving someone else.

Twenty-Six – Lady

It was a busy day at K&L Event Planning and I was sitting in my office when my door burst open. I damn near jumped out of the chair until I saw who it was. Sire was standing there looking a little off and I was wondering what the hell was wrong with him.

"What's—"

"Let's get married," he cut me off.

"We are getting married, Si. Did you forget?" I asked him as I held up the bridal magazines I was looking through.

"I mean now," he said.

"Now? What about my wedding and all this planning I been doing?" I asked confused.

"Just hear me out," he said as he walked closer to my desk. "Let's get married now down at the courthouse, but you can still plan your wedding and shit. We can have the big wedding later on down the road," he said.

I twisted my mouth to the side and thought about it for a second. It didn't sound like too bad of an idea to me. I was happy to know that he was anxious as hell to be my husband, because I was scared as hell his wishy washy ass might change his mind.

"What about our marriage license? We kind of need that to get married," I said.

"Well, see, if you had faith in your man, you would know that I already have it and the only thing we need to do is sign this muthafucka," he said, as he placed a manila folder on my desk.

I looked at him suspiciously before I reached for it and opened it. Sure enough, there was a marriage license with our names on it.

"Oh my God, when did you get this?" I laughed.

"I know somebody that knows somebody, who knows how to pull a few strings. Now that we got the license and shit, what you got to say?" he asked.

I sat there going over it in my mind. There was really nothing stopping us or holding us up from getting married now. Even though I still wanted my big wedding, I was fine with going to the courthouse to become Mrs. Kasire Lewis. Sire promised me that I could have my dream wedding as well, so I was going to hold him to it.

"Okay, let's do it," I said, finally.

"See, I thought I was going to have to drag yo' big headed ass out of here. I'm happy you choose the easy route though," he smiled, even though I knew he was serious.

"So when do I need to be ready so—"

"Now," he cut me off as he pulled me out of my chair.

"Now?" I exclaimed.

When he said let's get married now, I didn't actually think he meant now as in *right* now like today. I was sure he was going to say a week or two, but he sure as hell shamed the hell out of me.

"Why not, now?" he asked as he eyed me.

I didn't want him to get the notion that I was hesitant about marrying him or anything, so I decided to shut my mouth and go with the flow. No matter how crazy it might be.

"Nothing," I shook my head. "Let's go," I said.

The smile he had previously been wearing was back, and we were out the door. I made sure I closed and locked my office up and told my assistant to forward all the calls to my voicemail. I didn't know how long this would take or when I would be back. All I knew was I was becoming Mrs. Lewis today.

-$-

I stood in the bathroom of the courthouse staring in the mirror. *This is it*, I thought to myself. In just a few moments, I would officially be someone's wife. *Sire's* wife. After the life I lived, I never thought I would see this day. I honestly thought I would never be anything more than Omar's set-up bitch, but look at me now.

I wiped at the tears as they slowly fell from my eyes. For the first time in my life, I was truly happy.

"Now, now, Ms. Lady. We don't have all day," Mama Nisa said as she burst into the bathroom with my mom right on her heels.

"What…what are you two doing here?" I asked with a smile.

"Honey, now I know you don't think I would miss the day where my son would say 'I do' to somebody," Mama Nisa said.

"Lady, we need you to dry those tears and put this dress on. Per your husband's request," my mom said.

Husband, I smiled to myself. That just sounded so beautiful to me. My mouth fell open in amazement when my mom unzipped the garment bag she was carrying. In it was a beautiful white dress. It wasn't a wedding dress or anything of the sort, but it was beautiful nonetheless.

"Alright, we're going to get out of here so you can get dressed. Please don't keep that boy waiting any longer because he might kick this door in and pull you out," Mama Nisa smiled before kissing my cheek. "I always knew you were the one," she whispered in my ear as she pulled me in for a hug.

"Congratulations, baby, or should I say Mrs. Lewis," my mom said as she followed suit.

After they left, I wasted no time getting the dress on. I was so anxious that I could hardly contain myself. After getting dressed, I fixed my hair up a little before leaving the bathroom. When I walked out, Big R was standing by the door with his hands in his pockets.

"Hey you," I smiled. "What's wrong?" I asked when I noticed the look on his face.

"You look gorgeous. Lady, I know I'm not your father or anything, but I was wondering if I could do the honors of walking you to your husband?" he asked.

Oh gosh, here comes the waterworks. "I would be honored." I smiled, as I linked my arm with his.

My smile couldn't be contained as Big R and I walked through the courthouse doors. My heart instantly gushed when my eyes landed on Sire. He was standing there looking good as hell in a white linen suit that he had changed into. Big R walked me over to where we would be taking our vows, before he took his seat. That's when I noticed the whole family was there; literally the whole family, even the kids. Even Lace decided to show his face for the occasion, even though we weren't on the best of terms.

"Yo preach," Sire said to the officiant, "you mind if we cut out all the extra shit and get right to the 'I do's'?" he questioned.

If I was a couple of shades lighter, you would've been able to see my cheeks flush red from embarrassment. Sire was so antsy that he was doing the most right now.

"Si," I said through my teeth.

"What?" he asked as if he didn't know what he had done.

"It's alright," the officiant smiled. "I remember the feeling," he said.

I just shook my head because he thought Sire was joking, but I knew he was beyond serious. Sire wasn't going to be satisfied until we were officially married and the longer it took, the more restless he was going to be.

"Dearly beloved, we are gathered here today to witness the beautiful union of this young couple..."

I tuned the officiant out as I got lost in Sire's eyes. Through all the ups and downs we've been through, we were finally here. Getting married. I never thought I would see this day, but I'm blessed that I did.

"Kasire, do you take Lady to be your lawfully wedded wife? To have and to hold. To love and to cherish, in sickness and in health, for as long as you both shall—"

"I do!" Sire yelled. "I swear I do."

Everyone laughed and some cheered, even though we weren't done. Those that really knew Sire knew this was a big step for him.

"Well then, Lady—"

"She do, too," Sire cut the man off once again.

"Kasire, will you stop," I chuckled.

"Lady, do you take Kasire to be your husband? To have and to hold. To love and to cherish, in sickness and in health for as long as you both shall live?" he asked.

"I do," I said without any hesitation.

Before he could announce us as husband and wife, Sire took my face in his hands and gave me a big juicy kiss.

"By the power invested in me, I now pronounce you, husband and wife," he said.

The moment we all had been waiting for had finally come. We

were officially married and I was on a high that no drug could give me. Nothing or no one was going to be able to knock me off this cloud.

Charmanie Saquea

Twenty-Seven – Lala

"What did I do with that shirt?" I asked myself as I dug through clothes in my closet.

I had so many clothes in my closet that it was ridiculous. Every day I was in here looking for stuff and could never find it because I just had too much stuff. I was the type that went shopping every weekend, but claimed I had nothing to wear. If I wasn't buying clothes, I was spending my money on shoes or something for the kids. We all had a closet full.

"What the hell," I said when a big ass duffle bag fell off the shelf and damn near hit me in the head.

I looked at it odd because it didn't look familiar, nor did I remember placing it up there. When I unzipped it, my mouth fell open immediately. I was looking at enough evidence to get me sent away for a few lifetimes. I quickly zipped the bag back up before rushing out of the closet and grabbing my phone to call Toine up. I needed an explanation for this shit.

"Baby mama, what's up?" his happy go lucky ass answered the phone.

"Umm, Toine, when was the last time you were here?" I asked him.

"The other day, you know that. Why?" he asked.

"Did you forget a little something?"

"Forget what?" he questioned.

"Something in my closet that I can't say over the phone," I said through clenched teeth.

Never in all my years of knowing Toine had he ever thought to bring drugs around me or his kids, so the fact that he thought it would be okay to do it now was crazy. He could've at least gave me a heads up that he was leaving it here so that I would know and would be on the lookout just in case anything was to happen.

The line got quiet before Toine decided to speak again. "Get the fuck outta here, Alani!" his voice boomed as he caught my drift. "You know me, so you know I would never bring that shit around you or my damn kids. What type of nigga do you take me to be?" he yelled into the phone.

He was so loud that I had to remove the phone away from my ear and I could still hear him yelling. When I put the phone back up to my ear, he was still going off about this, that, and the other, but I cut him off.

"Okay, well if it wasn't you then who was it? I know Casper didn't walk his friendly ass in here and drop it off," I said.

"You right, Lala. Casper ain't do shit, but I need for you to stop playing dumb and acting like you don't know what the fuck is going on. It really ain't my business to tell, but if I were you, I would watch the company I lay down with," he said before hanging up on me.

I stood there looking at my phone, stuck on stupid. It wasn't even the fact that he had hung up on me because this wasn't the first time. It was what he was trying to insinuate that he me stuck. Had Darius been doing some shit right up under my nose and I had been playing blind to it? Now that I think about it, all of the signs had been there but I was paying them no attention. The late nights, him having more money to spend, being gone for days at a time but claiming he was staying at his house. I was no stranger to the shit because I had gone through it for years with Antoine.

The fact that Darius would be so disrespectful as to bring drugs where me and my children lay our heads at, was completely beyond me. He had me living in this fairytale world that he was a law abiding citizen that worked a good nine to five, when that couldn't have been further from the truth. Now, my ass was standing here looking stupid.

-$-

Later on that night, I played sleep in the bed when I heard

Darius come in the bedroom. Of course, he went straight for the closet and I already knew what his ass was looking for. After I'd finally had enough of him tearing up my damn closet, I crept out of the bed and pulled the bag from under my bed where I had previously hidden it.

"Looking for this?" I asked.

At the sound of my voice, Darius jumped before he turned around with a fake ass smile on his face. I stood there, stoned face, as I held the bag in my hands. He had been caught and he knew it.

"What you doing up?" he asked.

"What the fuck is this doing in my house and furthermore, what the fuck are you doing with it?" I yelled.

I thought I had given myself plenty of time to cool off, but obviously not. Just standing here confronting him about it was taking me to a whole other level. I had never been so pissed off or disrespected in my whole life. Not even with my dumb ass baby daddy and everybody knew nobody could get under my skin like Antoine could.

"I'm not about to do this with you right now, you tripping," he said, as he tried to reach for the bag.

"You damn right I'm tripping! Nigga, you got me fucked up to the highest point possible right now. You had the nerve to bring this shit here, where my kids are! Nigga, if it ever came down to it, I'm definitely choosing them over you! I would've sure as hell gave yo' ass up while you think you slick," I let him know.

Me saying that must have struck a nerve because I could see his breathing pick up and his fists ball up, but I didn't give a fuck. The only thing I knew how to be was real. If the police would've ran up in my shit because his stupid ass wanted to be deceitful and bring some drugs in a house he didn't even pay bills in, I would've sent them right in his direction. I'll be damned if I let any nigga make me fuck up my life over some stupid shit.

"Bitch, you—"

"Bitch?" I questioned. "The only bitch I see around here is you because you don't even know how to be grown about yours. Nigga, if I wanted to be with a weak ass dope boy, I could've stayed with Toine. At least he knew better than to pull some shit like this you—"

WHAP!

Before I even knew what the hell had happened, this nigga had slapped the fuck out of me, and had me pinned up against the dresser by my throat before I could react. His hold was so tight on my throat that I thought he was going to crush my windpipes. I

265

didn't even have the energy to fight him off.

"Bitch, fuck that soft ass nigga! Who the fuck you think I got the shit from? You so stuck up his ass that you don't even realize that nigga don't give a fuck about you," he spat. "That's okay though, because tomorrow his ass is going to be a dead nigga while he thinks he's going to be getting some money. I hope you enjoyed riding that nigga's dick while you could," he laughed menacingly.

That was all I heard before everything went black.

Twenty-Eight – Toine

I walked in the dark house and heard the familiar sound of a gun cocking before the cold metal was pressed to my head. A smile spread across my face before my arms slowly went up in the air. Under normal circumstances, I would've pulled my own firearm out and let off a shot, but this wasn't normal circumstances.

"It's me, Junior," I told my son.

"Dad?" AJ asked as he turned the light on. "My bad, I thought…" he stammered as he looked at me with horror in his eyes.

"It's cool. You did what you were supposed to do," I said, feeling like a proud parent as crazy as it sounds. "Where is she?" I asked as I took the gun from him.

"Still in the same spot," he said.

One of the worst things that could ever happen is getting a call from your son in the middle of the night that he's scared because his mom and her boyfriend are fighting. When AJ called to tell me that he saw Darius slap the fuck out of Lala and had her choked out in her room, I did about 80 getting here. I never thought I would've walked in to my son pointing a gun to my head, but he did the right thing. If Darius would've came back, he had the right to put a bullet in his ass.

I stopped by Antoinette's room and it was no surprise that her wild sleeping ass was still knocked out in her bed. After checking on her, I quickly rushed to Lala's room where she was still passed out on the floor from Darius's assault. My blood immediately started to boil when I saw the bruise that was forming on the side of her face.

"Junior, get me a cold rag," I instructed, as I lifted her off the floor and placed her on the bed.

I rubbed her hair until AJ came back with the cold rag for me to wipe her face with, as I tried to get her to wake up. I glanced over at my son as he worriedly looked at his mom. Looking at him reminded me of myself when I was his age. I would have the same look on my face when I looked over my mom whenever she came home high, and I would watch Anton try to sober her up. It happened so much that he just started to say fuck it and let her be.

While Anton grew up to have resentment and hate in his heart for our mama, I didn't love her any less. A lot of the problems my punk ass brother had in his life, stemmed from the issues had had with our daddy walking out of our life and our mama turning to drugs. Eventually she got clean, but by then, it was too late because she found out she had cancer before she succumbed to it.

"Come on, La," I coached as I lightly tapped her face.

"Is she okay?" AJ asked.

"Yea, she's good," I told him. "Ain't that right, La?" I asked her, as I continued to wipe her with the rag and tap her face.

After a few more minutes of that, she finally opened her eyes. She looked around the room as if she had to remember where she was at, before she tried to jump off the bed.

"Whoa, where the hell you going?" I asked.

"Oh my God! Toine, he said he was going to kill you!" she blurted out.

"What?" I laughed.

"Why you didn't tell me you were giving Darius drugs?" she asked.

I looked over at Junior and he quickly made his way out of the room. It wasn't like I hid anything from my kids, but I didn't think this was a conversation he needed to hear. He had already heard and seen enough for tonight.

"You bouncing around too much and not making any sense," I let her know.

"Well, apparently the drugs that I found belonged to Darius, which you already knew, but what he enlightened me on before he choked me out was that he got the drugs from you. So all this time you was supplying him and didn't bother to tell me?" she asked.

"First of all, that nigga ain't get shit from me. You know better than anybody that it's four of us niggas that work together, and I ain't never personally gave his ass shit. Yes, I could've let you know that nigga was a fraud, but would you have believed me? Like I told you earlier, it wasn't my place to say shit. You know who I was and what I was about from day one, I never hid it from you, so it was up to him to let you know what he was up to. Not me," I explained to her.

"Toine," Lala sighed as she ran her fingers through her hair. "I don't know what's supposed to be happening tomorrow, but I need for you to be careful. He said something about you, money, and him killing you. I don't know what he has up his sleeve, but I know you need to be on the lookout," she said.

"La, come on now, baby. You know who I am so you know that nigga is already a dead man walking. He signed his death certificate the second he thought it was okay to put his hands on you. I ain't worried about no nigga."

"No—"

"Shut up," I cut her off. "It's already done and ain't shit you can do about it. That nigga is as good as dead and I don't want to hear shit else about it. Now get the fuck up and let's go so we can go home," I said.

"Toine—"

"Do it look like this shit is up for debate?"

Lala rolled her eyes but I didn't give a fuck, because she got up like I told her to. This nigga was just making shit easier for me because I was coming to get my girl and kids anyways. Killing his stupid ass hadn't been a part of the plan, but I wasn't gon' complain about it.

-$-

I sat in the spot I was supposed to be meeting Darius to collect the money. It was funny to me that this nigga actually thought he was slick. He must have thought he was fucking with some average niggas or something. He was supposed to be originally meeting with Ry, but he suggested to meet with me instead because he claimed he had something to talk to me about, and this was the only time he could really reach me. This nigga was pulling rookie moves not knowing me and my niggas were already hip to the shit he was planning. He was crazy as fuck if he thought he could pull off a robbery on us. We had been in the game too long for some shit like this to be happening to us.

That nigga had better luck trying to break into the White House than trying to rob us.

Sire: *That dumb ass nigga pulling up now*

Sire had sent a text through a group message, alerting us that Darius was pulling up. He was posted up outside in a hidden spot with a sniper rifle, ready to let one off in Darius at any given moment. He was certified looney, but I loved that in him. Ry and Monty were also posted up in hidden locations, waiting to attack as well. Darius was so smart that he was dumb. If he had done his homework like he was supposed to, he would know what type of niggas he was dealing with and would know better than to cross us.

When he walked up, it took everything in me not to burst out laughing at him just for the simple fact that he was a sitting duck and didn't even know it. I was still trying to figure out what the hell Lala ever saw in his clown ass.

"Toine, what's up? Just the man I was looking for," Darius smiled, but it obviously didn't reach his eyes.

"Well you found me, nigga, not that that's really hard to do," I told him dryly.

I wasn't one for all the theatrics. He knew I ain't really cared

273

for his ass since day one, so there was no point in me standing here even trying to act cordial with his ass. I was really itching to put a bullet in his head as soon as he walked in, but that wouldn't have been smart of me. Or would it?

"I'm just gonna tell you like this since Lala really don't know how to tell you," he said as he clasped his hands together.

I stood there to hear whatever bullshit was about to come out of his mouth, because there wasn't shit he had to tell me when it came to her, but I damn sure did have a mouthful to tell him.

"Tell me then, nigga."

"Alani and I are getting married. I'm sure you don't know because she didn't want to hurt your feelings, considering the fact that you won't leave her alone and all that. So, I decided to come to you man to man and let you know that whatever feelings you may have for her, you need to let them go," he said.

That was when I couldn't hold it any longer. I burst into laughter right in his face at his pitiful ass. I guess he really didn't know Lala like he thought he did. He was one dumb ass nigga if he thought for one second that I believed anything that was coming out of his mouth.

"You right, she didn't have time to tell me between our

countless lovemaking sessions. It must have just slipped her mind the same way this dick slips in and out of her." I smirked at the priceless look on his face. "Yea, nigga, all those nights your fake ass was working late, we be spending family time together, with *our* kids. While you thought you had her, a real nigga had her heart the whole time. Congratulations, you played yourself."

That night I got the call about Antonia and Andre being at the police station, was the first night that Lala and I had been together since our breakup. She tried to hold strong and play 'faithful' to this fuck nigga, but she knew just like I knew that nobody knows or can do her body like me. I'm a persistent ass nigga who doesn't stop until I get what I want. That night, I got my girl back, and this nigga didn't even know it.

I guess this nigga couldn't handle the truth because he called himself trying to pull a gun out on me. If only he knew, one of us surely wasn't making it out of here alive, and that one wasn't going to be me.

"You that mad, nigga?" I smiled.

"Say the word, Toine," Ry said as he walked in.

He distracted Darius, causing him to turn his head which was a wrong move on his part, because I reached behind me for my gun, pressing it against his head.

"It's cool, Ry. This one is mine," I said as I reached in my pocket for my phone.

"Hello?" a groggy sounding Lala answered the phone as I put it on speaker.

"Bae, you trust me?" I asked with my eyes trained on Darius, who was so mad he could spit bullets.

"What? Yea, of course I do," she said.

"So you know that any problem that you have, I'll take care of it like it's mine."

The line was quiet before she spoke again. "Yes, I know."

"I love you, Alani."

"I love you too, Antoine. Make it home safe," she said.

I smiled before hanging up and pulling the trigger at the same time. While I was stuffing my phone in my pocket, his body fell to the ground with a hard thud. *My job here is done,* I thought, as I stepped over him as if he wasn't even there.

"Gentlemen, this was fun, but until next time…" I said.

"Yo' trigger happy ass always taking the fun out of something," Ry complained.

I just hit him with a smile as I made my way home to be with my woman and my kids. It felt good to be able to say that shit again after two years. Just like I knew we would, Lala and I were back on track, and this time, wasn't shit going to fuck up our union.

Charmanie Saquea

Twenty-Nine – Sire

"Ooh, Sire…damn," Lady moaned as she tried to run from the dick.

I don't know what it was, but it was something about being married that had us fucking like rabbits lately, especially today. Toine and Lala were being some nice little hosts and were having the sleepover of a lifetime, and invited everybody's kids over. So, Lady and I decided to take full advantage of having the house to ourselves.

I had her bent over the bed, stuffing her with dick, but she wanted to act like she couldn't take it.

"You better stay here and take this dick, girl."

"Sire, wait," she said as she tried to stand up.

"Wait my ass," I said as I pushed her back down on the bed.

"No, Sire. I'm for real. Did you hear that?" she asked as she tried to push me off of her.

"The only thing I'm trying to hear is my balls slapping against that fat ass."

"Come on now, Kasire. I'm not playing. I know I heard something so cut it out and take me serious right now."

I let out a growl as I reluctantly pulled out of her to see what the hell was going on just to appease her. When I was walking to the closet and she was headed to the bathroom, I finally heard whatever noise she was talking about. She gave me a look as to say 'I told yo' ass' while throwing her robe on.

I grabbed my gun because whoever the fuck had the balls to be in my house was going to be met with an untimely death. Not only were they in my shit unwelcomed, but they were fucking up me getting some pussy. While I was throwing some pants on, I looked out the corner of my eye to see Lady doing something. When I turned around, I saw her cocking my other gun like she was really about to do something.

"Ready," she said.

I stood looking at her with a blank expression because the only thing she was ready for was to get her fucking head knocked off.

"What the fuck I tell you about that playing gangster shit? Sit yo' goofy ass down somewhere before you make me cuss you out," I snapped.

She pouted, but did as she was told and walked back in the closet to put my gun back. I just shook my head as I made my way out of my room with my gun right by my side. When I reached the stairway, these dumb muthafuckas were making their way up.

280

POW, POW!

Hitting both of my targets, I let off two shots that would be good enough to take them down but not kill them. I needed answers, so I was going to let them live... for the moment. They both fell back down the stairs and landed on the bottom with hard thuds.

I jogged down the stairs and aimed my gun at one of their heads, while I turned the light on.

"Who sent you?"

The stupid ass niggas didn't even bother to have masks on.

"Sire?" he asked as if he knew he had fucked up. "Aw, damn. That nigga ain't tell us it was you," he said.

POW!

I sent another bullet into his kneecap because he wasn't saying shit I needed to hear.

"Aww fuck!" he yelled out in agony.

"Speak," I told his friend.

"Lace...it was this nigga named Lace!" he yelled out. "He owed us a debt for gambling, but instead of paying up, he gave us the address where he said he knew somebody had the cash stashed.

He never mentioned the fact that it was you though, Sire. We don't even know how you know that nigga. I swear to God," he said with his hands up as he laid on the ground.

"It's cool," I shrugged.

I quickly put a bullet in his friends head before putting one in his head. They had to be stupid to think that I would let them live to tell that they broke into my shit and tried to rob me. They surely had me fucked up.

"AHH!"

I turned around and looked at the top of the stairs where Lady was standing with her mouth covered. I was sure she heard the whole conversation, so she knew her brother wasn't shit. If looks could kill, her ass would've dropped dead too.

I walked back up the stairs so I could call the clean-up crew. I didn't even bother saying anything to her because if I did, it most likely would've been the wrong thing. Even though I shouldn't have, I was putting this one on her. It was her grimy ass brother that sent these muthafuckas to rob us, and they possibly could've killed us.

Had she not brought this nigga to my humble abode, we never would've had to worry about no shit like this. She should've just left his ignorant ass right where the fuck she found him. In Detroit. Now his blood was about to be on her hands.

"Si—"

"Not right now," I snapped. "Not the fuck right now!"

I was so pissed off that I could kill me a nigga, and that nigga was going to be her punk ass excuse of a brother. At first, I was all for her finding him because I was trying to play the supportive role, but the moment I actually laid eyes on this nigga, I knew he wasn't shit. My suspicions were just further being confirmed.

After I was finished getting dressed, I looked up to find Lady sitting on the bed, silently crying. I wanted to console her, but I couldn't. She already knew what the outcome of this situation was going to be, and I didn't have any words to comfort her. What could you say to your wife, knowing you were on your way to kill her brother? Not a damn thing.

-$-

I didn't have to put too much effort into looking for the dumb fuck. Ry and I hit up a place that was notorious for its underground gambling ring, and guess who we just happened to find standing outside. It was a Friday night so the place was booming.

"This nigga really had the nerve to set up his own sister?" Ry asked in disbelief. "Never mind the fact that you live there too, but his own sister? And he knows his niece and nephews lay they head there and anything could've happened to them." He shook his head.

That was the part that I was stuck on. This wasn't the first robbery attempt I had ever gone through, but you had to be one very fucked up individual to set up your own sister to be robbed.

"That's that fuck nigga mentality," I said, as I kept my eye trained on him while we continued to sit in the car.

"I told sis she didn't know that nigga. Ever since his bitch ass popped up in the picture, our relationship has been real off and I ain't feeling the shit," Ry hawked.

I know baby bro had to be feeling some type of way. Before Lady even knew this nigga existed, her and Ry were tight as fuck. I mean, the shit was to the point that it got on my fucking nerves, even though I knew there wasn't shit I could do about it. Then all of a sudden, in walks this nigga and Lady was acting as if she just had to give him all of her attention. Ry didn't say anything, at least no to her, because he was trying to make it seem as if he was very understanding of the situation, when I couldn't give a fuck less.

"Well, after tonight you won't have to worry about this shit no more. Let's go," I said as we got out of the car.

As we walked in Lace's direction, he didn't even look as if he was shocked that I was even there. This nigga even had the audacity to be smirking at me before he took a puff of his cigarette.

"To what do I owe the pleasure?" he asked.

I hauled off and hit him dead in his shit before pulling my gun out and slapping him in the head with it.

"The pleasure's about to be all mine, bitch," I spewed.

The dice game that was going on a few feet away, quickly dissipated when they saw what was about to go down. I wasn't worried about nobody saying shit or calling the law, because most of these cats knew me and what I was about.

As if I thought this nigga was crazy before, his ass started laughing as he wiped the blood from his mouth. Ry looked at me like he didn't know what the fuck to do, but I was unfazed. This nigga may have *thought* he was crazy, but he was no match for my crazy.

"You would really kill your wife's brother? How do you think that would make her feel?" he fake pouted.

"You crazy as fuck if you think I give a fuck. Just like you ain't give a fuck how she would feel when you sent them niggas to run up in our shit," I told him.

"I—"

POW!

"Ahhh, fuck!" he yelled as he grabbed for the bullet wound in his side.

"Look, bitch, this is how the fuck this shit is going to go," I said, as I grabbed his stupid ass up by his collar. "You're going to use whatever money you won from here to buy you a one-way ticket back to Detroit. You're going to stay the fuck away from Lady and her mom, and if I even just think you tried to contact her or even feel like you're still in my city, next time this bullet is going to be going in your fucking head," I snarled, before shoving him away.

Ry looked at me like he couldn't believe what the fuck was going on, as I made my way back to the car. I heard him running to catch up with me and knew he was about to say something stupid.

"You know that nigga still breathing, right?" he asked as he got in the car.

It never fails, I thought, as I barely waited for him to shut the door before I sped away. Out the corner of my eye, I could see him staring at me before a smile spread across his face.

"In the name of love," he said. "Let me find out being married done made yo' ass soft."

I grumbled at those words because that would never be my story. Yes, what I did tonight by letting Lace live might have had something to do with Lady, but by no means was I getting soft. I just didn't want to have to look her in the eye and tell her I killed her hoe ass brother. Now, had she been any other bitch, I clearly wouldn't have given one fuck, two fucks, red fucks, blue fucks. But it was Lady…my wife.

When I got home, Lady was sitting in the bed waiting for me to get home. The clean-up crew had long since came and gone, and you couldn't even tell that it had been a double murder scene a few hours earlier. I didn't say anything to her or bother to turn on the lights as I walked to the closet to get undressed.

"Did you kill him?" she asked.

I didn't answer her immediately. Instead, I stripped down to my boxers and climbed under the sheets, lying with my hands in back of my head.

"I should've," I finally said.

I heard Lady let out a breath of air she probably had been holding since she asked her question. She scooted down in the bed and laid her hands on my chest, before snuggling up close to me. I had to chuckle at the fact that Ry thought me being married was making me soft. That wasn't possible…or was it?

Thirty – Lady

"I need those flower arrangements delivered no later than one o'clock tomorrow," I instructed as I walked in the house.

I tried hard to not bring my work home with me, but I had a really big event that I had to plan and my clients gave me little to no time to do so. I wasn't going to complain though, because this was my job and this was what I loved to do.

When I walked into my living room, instead of being greeted by my rowdy kids, I was greeted by some bitch that I had never seen before. I had to stop and look around to make sure I didn't walk in the wrong house by accident, because this hoe was looking real comfortable.

"Who are you?" I asked, not hiding the attitude in my voice.

"Atalia," she answered.

"Okay? And?" I asked.

This bitch just sat here with a blank expression on her face like she didn't understand what the fuck I was saying to her, so I was going to see if she understood what the fuck a fist felt like.

"Yooo, Lady!" Ry yelled as he walked in the room. "What you doing here?" he asked as he stood in front of me to stop me from walking up on the girl.

"Nigga, I live here. Who the fuck is this?" I reiterated with more attitude than I did the first time.

"Sis, I'm so happy to see you. I swear it feels like forever since the last time we kicked it," he smiled before he hugged me. "Lady, please keep calm and allow Sire to explain everything," he whispered in my ear.

I stepped back and looked at him like he had lost his mind. I was sure that he had, because there was no way in hell he was telling me to keep calm while he and his brother had some random ass bitch in my house, and had yet to explain to me who she was.

"Kasire!" I yelled, letting all that keep calm shit go out the window. "Where the fuck are my kids, and I'm not going to ask again who this bitch is that y'all got in my house!"

"Bitch?" she asked like she had a problem.

As soon as I heard her open her mouth, I turned around to get her ass. I was the queen of this castle and I wasn't feeling the shady shit that was going on. Before I could even take another step, I was swooped up from behind.

"I told yo' stupid ass to sit here and not say shit. Shut the fuck up!" Sire's voice boomed from behind me as he carried me out of the room.

He didn't put me down until we got into the kitchen and I didn't try to hide the attitude I had as I crossed my arms over my chest.

"Be mad at Ry's simple ass. He's the one who brought her over here," he said.

"Y'all still not saying who the fuck she is. Let me fucking find out," I accused without having to say too much.

"See, now you doing too much. That bitch in there don't mean shit to me and ain't meant shit to me in years. I ain't gone lie to you, when I was a young and dumb ass teenager, I thought she was going to be the one until she crossed me. Now, here she is years later, needing my help," he half-ass explained.

"Help with what?" I questioned.

"Her brother was this grimy ass nigga that I used to do business with. He used to do some wild and crazy ass shit to her. I mean, some shit a brother should never do to his own sister. Well, the nigga is out of prison now and coming after her to hurt her, and she needs my help getting rid of him for good."

I stood there looking at Sire like he was stupid. I was sure there was a lot of stuff that he was leaving out, but I didn't even care about all that. I was tripping off of the fact that he just stood here and told me out his own mouth that this bitch had crossed him, but in the same breath told me he was going to help her.

"That's not your problem, get rid of the bitch," I said in a flat tone before trying to turn around.

"Lady, I—"

"If it was Lexus, would you do it?" I threw at him.

"Fuck nah, why would you even ask me some shit like that?"

"Hell, Lexus crossed you and every time you saw her it was nothing but bad blood between the two of you. Yet, this bitch crossed you and you wanna be her superman. Help me understand the difference between the two," I said, truly confused.

I really didn't want to jump to conclusions, but I know when some shit wasn't right. Call me crazy, but that bitch in that other room wanted more than for Sire to just save her as she claimed.

"Don't do that, okay? You making shit bigger than what it needs to be. All I'm doing is getting rid of this nigga then sending her on her way. I already told you that damn girl don't mean shit to me," he said.

I didn't even bother to say anything else to Sire because it wouldn't have done any good. Sire was the type where you could talk to him until you were fucking blue in the face, but he would still do whatever the hell he wanted to do. All I know was, all three of them had me fucked up, Ry included.

If he couldn't see what the hell was going on with this damn girl, it's because he didn't want to see it. A blind man could see that damn girl still wanted Sire. All I know was she better stay in her fucking lane because I wasn't about to play with her ass.

-$-

There had been so much tension in my house that I was happy to have some much needed girl time with Lala, Tracy, Tasha, Cola, and even Candace. The more I stayed in the house with Sire, the more I wanted to knock him over the damn head.

"So what's been going on with you, Mrs. Newlywed?" Tasha asked. "We haven't been seeing too much of you," she said as she got her toes done.

The six of us were spending the day at the spa, getting some much needed relaxation, since we all spent the day running after kids on top of working jobs. Candace was the only one who didn't have kids, but that didn't mean she doesn't work as hard as the rest of us.

"That's because I'm about to become Mrs. Widow," I huffed.

"Oh Lord. What's wrong? Y'all ain't even been married a month and you talking about killing the man," Lala giggled.

"This bitch named Atalia is what's wrong," I spat.

"Who?" everybody asked, except for Tasha and Cola, who both gave each other a look.

"Where did that bitch crawl out from?" Cola asked with her face scrunched up.

I damn near broke my neck looking in her direction when she said that. I almost forgot that she had been around the fellas since forever, so she most likely knew who this bitch was. I had to get my cup ready because I needed all the tea she was about to spill.

"So you know her?" I asked through squinted eyes. "You too, Tasha?" I questioned.

"Not necessarily. I heard of her, but didn't really have the pleasure of meeting her. I know she was responsible for Sire getting locked up for the first time," Tasha shrugged.

"That is true," Cola confirmed.

"Okay, Cola Bear. I need you to spill it because my husband seems to think he doesn't have to give me any details on the bitch," I told her.

"Honestly, Lady, I'm surprised Sire hasn't put a bullet in her. Sire was in love with that girl. I mean whenever you saw Sire, there was Tali. She used to go on runs with Sire, package, cut, count his money, all of that. She was a real ride or die…so we thought. Her brother used to work with Sire, but he had some screws missing. He used to rape her and beat her ass like crazy, and she told Sire about it. They came up with this plan to kill Akil, but Atalia froze up and worked with her brother to set Sire up to get sent to prison. I'm not sure how the roles reversed and she ended up working with the wrong nigga, but Sire was beyond pissed. He told Monty and Ry to send a message to Atalia that she had to leave Richmond and she'd better not come back, or he was going to kill her. Nobody had heard from her since, and that was years ago," Cola explained.

By the time she was done, all of us were sitting there in shock. I thought Lexus was a grimy bitch, but this one here took the cake. These two hoes were the reason I had to go through so much hell with Sire in our relationship. He didn't know if my intentions with him were good because every bitch before me had did him dirty.

"That's deep," Lala said.

"Very," Tracy agreed.

"Nah, what's deep is this brother is apparently coming after her ass, and Sire wants to play captain save-a-hoe," I announced.

"I don't know, Lady. I honestly wouldn't trust the bitch, and I damn sure wouldn't trust my husband around her. I'm not saying you can't trust Sire, but it's her you can't trust," Cola informed me.

"I'm already hipped, Cola. I saw it in the way she sat on my couch like she had some type of power or something. What I want to know is why all these years later would she want to come to Sire to help her ass? Why not go to the police if you're scared of this nigga?"

"You know what I think?" Lala asked as she flipped her hair. "I think we need to do a little digging on this bitch. Lady is right, something ain't adding up."

"Oh Lord," Candace said.

I smiled because Lala was on to something. I needed to do my own research on the bitch that Sire felt so compelled to help out. I wouldn't even be mad, if I didn't feel like there was some underhanded sneaky shit going on.

Charmanie Saquea

Thirty-One – Monty

"Daddy look! I made a sand castle!" Nylah yelled with excitement.

I had decided to spend a weekend with my girls in Virginia Beach, and take them swimming on the oceanfront. Today was our first day here, and so far, we had been having nothing but fun.

"When you gonna give me another one?" I asked Cola as she took a seat next to me in the sand.

"Another what?" she asked clueless.

"Kid."

Lately, things had been going smoothly in our relationship. There hadn't been any fighting, only minor disagreements that we were able to sit down and work out before the day was over. She didn't complain about my choice of career anymore, and had even applied for a job as a physical therapist.

"Another kid, huh? Are we ready for that?" she asked.

"Yea, why wouldn't we be?" I asked.

I loved having Nylah around and no DNA test could tell me if she was mine or not. I was all she knew and all she needed to know. Even with that, I couldn't help but to feel like I wanted another child. Nylah was six years old now and I felt like I had missed out on some of the best years of her life, with us meeting for the first time when she was four years old.

"What about marriage?" Cola asked.

My eyes bucked because that shit had really just come out of left field. I don't know how we just went from talking about having another child to her bringing up marriage.

"What about it?" I asked.

"You don't ever want to be married?" Cola asked.

"No...I mean...yea...I mean, I don't know," I stammered.

Cola was really throwing me now and I didn't know what to say. I was still young so marriage really wasn't on my mind. Right now, I was just trying to stack my paper and take care of my family so I could give them everything I had to go without.

Cola looked at me for a second, before putting her eyes back on Nylah, who was having the time of her life playing in the sand.

"What Sire and Lady have, I want that. I want to be married one day. I don't want to be just another baby mama. You know? I want to be someone's wife," she said.

I blame this shit on Sire. He was going around having

weddings and shit so it had the rest of the women in the family looking at us niggas, wondering when they were going to get a ring. Don't get me wrong, I think it's a beautiful thing that he decided that Lady was the woman that he wanted to spend the rest of his life with and had no problems locking that down, but I didn't want to feel like I was rushing into anything.

I'm not saying that I couldn't see me being with Cola for the rest of my life, I would love that. I just didn't know if that marriage shit was for me.

"Um…well…"

"Calm down, Bear. I'm not asking you to marry me or anything like that. I'm just saying that the way Nylah was conceived was far from ideal. The next child that I bring into this world, I want it to be with love. I don't know, I guess I'm just scared," she sighed, as she played with her hands.

"You don't think I love you?"

"I don't have any doubts that you do, but what if we don't work out? That'll leave me with two kids that I have to raise on my own," she said.

I looked at Cola with my face scrunched up because none of what she was saying was making sense to me.

"Where the hell you getting this shit from? You sound crazy if you think I would ever leave you out here hurting while you got my kids. You know me better than that, so you know that as long as you got Ny, you gon' be straight regardless."

"You remember Darren?" she asked.

I had to think on it for a little while, but then it hit me that he was the little nigga that had followed her up here from Texas and got mad when she didn't want to be with her.

"Yea, what he got to do with us?" I asked, wondering why she was bringing him up.

"He told me once that no one was going to want me, that my life was basically screwed and that I would always be left to raise my daughter by myself. He—"

"Nicola, cut all that shit out, okay? This is the same nigga that threw a bitch fit because you wouldn't give him no pussy. Shouldn't nobody want yo' ass but me, flat out. We gon' be together until I'm old, wrinkly, and got grey hairs on my balls," I told her.

Cola laughed as she laid her head on my shoulder. "I love your crazy ass."

"I love you, too, but don't think you off the hook. I still want

302

me a son, nigga," I nudged her head.

"I hear you," she said.

"I don't want you to hear me, I want you to feel me," I told her, as I placed her hand on my dick.

"You are so nasty; your daughter is over there," she giggled.

"She ain't worried about us. She over there building ugly ass sand castles and shit."

Cola just shook her head with a smile, as she pulled my face in to give me a kiss.

"Ewe, y'all nasty," we heard, followed by giggling.

I looked out the corner of my eye to see Nylah running towards us. She sat in between the middle of Cola and I with the biggest smile on her face. I just shook my head at her. We were definitely going to have to put in overtime to give her a brother or sister to play with, because I wasn't for all this cock blocking my child was doing.

Charmanie Saquea

Thirty-Two – Toine

"Your honor, my client has more than a substantial amount of evidence to prove that not only is he capable of taking care of his son, but that he's been doing so without even being able to see him," Tracy said as she held up a folder.

Today was my court date with Alisha's trifling ass and for some reason, I was more nervous than a prostitute in church. Of course, I had my queen here by my side to show her support and to let me know that everything was going to be okay. On top of that, I had Tracy going to bat for a nigga and doing what she did best in the courtroom.

"Let me see," the judge said.

Tracy walked up to the bench and handed him the two folders that contained all the receipts and everything else that I kept in regards to what I have bought for my son. Usually, I wouldn't even do no shit like this, but something told me to keep track of everything, and I'm happy I did.

"When was the last time you saw your son, Mr. Matthews?" the judge asked.

"It's been almost three months, your honor," I said, as I cut my eyes at Alisha's stupid ass.

"Is that true, Ms. Manor?" he asked Alisha as he looked over his glasses.

"Yes, but he—"

"I didn't ask for an explanation, I just asked if it was true or not," he said.

"Yes," she mumbled.

"Your honor, if I may," her lawyer said.

"You may," the judge said like he really didn't want to hear it, but was going to let him go ahead anyways.

"Your honor, my client has expressed some worries about the company that the defendant keeps. She had great concerns about the many women that he has around her son and fears that they might try to harm her child," his doofus ass had the nerve to say.

"How can I have him around women when I don't even get to see him?" I snapped.

This was some bullshit and I wasn't about to play with her stupid ass, especially when it came to my child. She was playing a very dangerous game that was putting her life in danger. I don't give a fuck whose mama she is, all bets are off the table when it comes to my child.

"Calm down, let me handle this," Tracy whispered in your ear. "Your honor, I would like to speak on that. As my client stated, he hasn't been able to see his son in months and even when he was able to see him, Ms. Manor always gave him a hard time. He has no women cycling around, in fact, he has a fiancé that he's been with for years. Yes, they took a little break, but they are very happy right now. She had kids of her own with my client and is very active in his other children's lives, so I highly doubt she would have a reason to hurt her son," Tracy stated.

I smiled to myself because Tracy was right on the ball. Not only did Alisha have me fucked up, but she had Lala fucked up as well. The only person who had ever been around my kids was Lala. Whenever we were on breaks, my kids never knew because she was always around and always in their lives, like Tracy stated. They didn't even know about Alisha until we found out her son was mine. Hell, they still don't know about her because she did her best to keep my son away from us with her stupid ass.

"I see," the judge said as he nodded his head.

With that, Alisha and her lawyer were both left standing there looking stupid. I couldn't even believe that she would even try to use that bullshit about our son not being safe to justify her reasoning from keeping him away from me. The bitch was just bitter and I couldn't believe that I had even gotten caught up with her stupid ass.

-$-

"I know it probably didn't go exactly how you wanted, but at least you have joint custody of little man," Lala said as we were leaving the courthouse.

Lala was right. This shit didn't go how I wanted to because Alisha was granted this child support shit, and she was going to use that bullshit just to think she had me by the balls. Little did she know, she had another thing coming.

"Well, well, well, if it isn't the, wait—what she called y'all…happy couple, right?" we heard from behind us.

I had to laugh because this bitch just didn't know when to leave well enough alone. I don't know why she couldn't see that she was barking up the wrong tree. I really had gotten rid of Heaven's ass just to end up with one just like her bitter ass. Just younger and dumber.

"Bitch—"

"Nah, baby, it's cool," Lala said as she pulled me behind her. "I got it."

"Got what? Last time I checked, you were so threatened by me that you left his ass, now all of a sudden you wanna play the role of

308

the happy girlfriend." Alisha rolled her eyes.

"Threatened? By you? Baby girl, Alani could never be threatened by you or any other bitch for that matter. What he do, fuck you in one of those rooms at that three-star hotel you work at, and the dick was so good that you had to think of a way to trap his ass? Thinking that a baby would keep him around and started feeling stupid when you realized you would never be *the* one. Just one of many. Yea, bitch, I know how the game go. I've come across plenty of bitches like you, and guess who's still here standing tall," Lala chuckled.

I covered my mouth to stifle my laugh because Lala was right. I did fuck Alisha in one of the rooms at her job. That was actually the first day I met her, when Lala wasn't giving me no play. I was supposed to be on a mission but I saw her, spit my game, then next thing I knew, I had her sneaking off on her shift and had her bent over the bed in one of the rooms.

"Bitch, so what you—"

"Nah, you've said enough. Too much actually," Lala cut her off. "The best thing for you to do right now would be to walk away while you still can, because it's taking everything in me not to hit you in yo' shit. Be sure to give my stepson a kiss for me, and tell him daddy will be on his way to get him later," Lala blew a kiss at her before turning around.

Hand in hand, we walked away together, leaving Alisha standing there feeling stupid. This was why I loved Lala. No matter what, she always had a nigga's back. We may have had our ups and downs, but she never let that get in the way of what really mattered.

Thirty-Three – Ry

I walked in Candace's new house to help her move in, but was greeted by the sounds of laughter and a familiar voice. When I walked around the corner, I stood there with a dumbfounded look on my face at the sight before me.

"Hi, Daddy," Ryley said.

Tasha and Candace both looked at me before looking at each other and laughing. I stood there stuck because I really was confused as to what the hell was going on.

"What the fuck is going on?" I asked.

"Ohh, Daddy, you say bad word," Ryley reminded me.

"Sorry, baby girl, daddy's just confused," I said as I stood there, still stuck.

"Ry, while you're standing there, can you hand me that box next to you?" Candace asked.

Finally willing myself to move, I picked the box up and took it to her. When I reached her, she and Tasha were just full of giggles.

"Why are you here? How do you even know her?" I asked Tasha.

"Lady introduced us," she stuck her tongue out. "I like her, Ryan, why you been hiding her from me?"

"Because of shit like this!" I exclaimed.

"Daddy!"

Tasha took some newspaper she had balled up and threw it at my head before rolling her eyes.

"Your daughter is going to beat you up," Candace laughed.

"Candy, are you okay? Did she drug you? Are you scared? Blink once for yes."

I don't know what the hell they thought this was so funny when I was serious as hell. Shit like this wasn't normal for me. I didn't know how to feel about this one right here. I knew I told Tasha that I would eventually introduce her to Candace but I didn't think it would be this soon. I thought it would be a little later on down the line when we were all a little bit more comfortable with the situation, even the fact that Ryley was in here chilling with Candace had me puzzled.

"Why you acting like that? I told you I like her," Tasha said.

"Yea, why you act like it's such a bad thing for us to get to know each other and hang out?" Candace asked.

"It is. You two are supposed to be at odds and fighting in the streets somewhere. Where I'm from, shit like this is not normal. The baby mama is not supposed to like the new girl. This some twilight zone shit y'all trying to do," I said.

"No, this is some grown woman stuff we're doing here. Why would I try to fight her or hate her when me and you have nothing going on? If she's going to be around you that mean she's going to be around my daughter, so I have to at least get to know her. I know you, so I know you wouldn't just be with anything. We spent some time together and I like her, she was cool and down to earth. I can admit if this was about five years ago, then maybe I wouldn't be able to do this, but I'm mature now. I'm just trying to help make your life less stressful," Tasha explained.

"She's right, Ry. We are too grown to be hating each other. She already assured me that there was nothing going on between the two of you but Ryley, and that you were very good friends," Candace shrugged with a smile.

When I sat there and thought about it, it did sound good as hell. While everybody else was going through drama with the women in their lives, I could live a peaceful life because all my girls got along. I was basically living the dream.

"Y'all right, my bad."

"Now, let's talk business," Tasha said.

"Here you go, what now?" I asked.

"Why would you bring that girl back into Sire's life, knowing Lady was going to flip out?" she asked with her hands on her hips.

I shook my head because once again, Lady and I were on the outs. She was so pissed off at me that she wasn't talking to me at all, and even Sire had beef with me because his wife was mad at him. He was blaming me for her holding out on the pussy, having attitudes, and giving him the silent treatment. I felt like I didn't have shit to do with that.

"Look, Atalia called me up crying about how this nigga was terrorizing her and she was scared to do anything and all that good shit. The only reason I told Sire was because I know he got a personal beef with Akil and wants him dead. I figured it would be a win-win situation for the both of them. Never did I expect for it, nor did I intentionally try to cause problems in their marriage. That ain't me, and I would never do that. I love the both of them too much for that."

"But you had to know that Lady would feel some type of way though, Ry. This is Sire's ex. Not just any ex, but his first love," Candace said.

"Yea, I know, but damn. I honestly didn't think he would even want shit to do with her after what she did to him. Sire loved that damn girl and she did him wrong as fuck, like very wrong. I know he wouldn't be stupid enough to fuck up what he got with Lady for her shady ass," I said.

Atalia is a part of Sire's past that he rarely even speaks about. The love they had for each other could be described as some kiddie, puppy love type shit. Sire was a grown man so I highly doubt he would want anything to do with her. If he had common sense, he wouldn't.

"All I'm saying is home girl better watch her back because Lady is gunning for her. A woman knows when a bitch wants her man. She can play that sob, sorry, damsel in distress role and fool y'all, but she ain't fooling none of us. If she thought somebody was after her before, let her fuck with Sire and see if Lady really don't come after her ass," Tasha said.

"You crazy, Atalia ain't thinking about Si," I waved her off.

"Humph," Candace said as she opened up a box and started pulling stuff out.

I didn't know what the hell they had going on, but they were tripping. It had been years since Atalia and Sire had even last laid eyes on each other, so I'm sure the feelings between the two of them had died long ago.

Charmanie Saquea

Thirty-Four – Sire

Me: *I'll be home in a minute. I got some shit I need to take care of. I love you.*

I kept checking my phone for a reply but one never came through. I had sent that message a whole half hour ago but yet, Lady wasn't fucking with me. She had been in her feelings lately, and I hated the shit. Ever since I had come home from prison, we had been doing good and been happy as hell. Now we were starting back with the unnecessary bullshit.

"She's a lucky girl."

I lifted the bottle of Hennessey up to my lips and took a big chug of it as I looked at Atalia like I wanted to slap her ass. Her stupid ass was the reason I was even having problems with my wife. If she would've just stayed the fuck away like I told her to, I wouldn't even be going through this shit.

"Yea, she knows she got a good thing and would never do shit to fuck it up. I don't ever have to worry about her crossing me. Realest bitch I've ever come across."

Just thinking about the bullshit Atalia did to me had me wanting to go upside her head since I never got a chance to all those years ago. I never thought I would see the day where she

319

would pull a move so grimy as to set me up with the same nigga she was supposed to be so fucking scared of.

"Here we go with this again," she sighed. "How many times do you want me to apologize, Sire? I told you I didn't have a choice because he was going to kill me. You—"

"I don't wanna hear that shit!" my voice boomed. "You know damn well I wouldn't have let that nigga do shit to you. You did that shit because you wanted to. I should've known you wasn't 'bout shit from the jump. That was my bad, though."

"I wasn't about shit? Are you serious right now, Sire? I was there for you before the money and all the hood fame! I was the one who was there when you couldn't sleep at night because you was having nightmares about that nigga beating yo' ass! Not that bitch you fucking married but me!" she yelled.

It seemed as if Atalia knew she fucked up as soon as the words left her mouth. She stood there covering her mouth with wide eyes as if she wasn't supposed to say that shit. It was too late now. There was no coming back from that shit.

"Sire, I'm sorry. I didn't—"

"The best thing for you to do right now is to shut the fuck up talking to me while you still can, before I snap yo' fucking neck," I said, with nothing but ice dripping from my veins.

I wasn't even tripping over the fact that she brought that shit up. I was pissed the fuck off because she thought it was okay to use that shit against me. Besides Lady, she was the only person outside of my family who really knew about my past abuse as a child. I thought I was going to spend the rest of my life with this girl, so I had no problems telling her. Yet, here she was using the shit to try and hurt me.

I had to take another swig from the bottle in my hands because this was the only thing helping me calm my nerves right now. This bitch was about to make me kill her ass and my wife was giving me her ass to kiss because she was mad at a nigga. I shouldn't even be here in the first place, but I was on a mission to kill a nigga and Atalia was the only person who could lead him right to me.

"Look, Si," she said, not knowing when to leave well enough alone. "I know you probably hate my guts and I can't say that I blame you, but I really am sorry. You don't know how much I regret doing what I did. You were the only person who had my back when even my own parents said to hell with me. I know my words don't hold weight with you anymore, but if I could go back and do things differently, I would."

The more she talked the more I drank. I just needed this nigga to show up so I can do what the fuck I gotta do so I can get the fuck away from this broad. I would rather be at home chasing after my bad ass kids, or laid up in Lady's wet ass pussy, than to be here dealing with her bullshit.

-§-

"Fuck," I groaned at the throbbing feeling in my head.

I had to grab my head in my hands because the room was literally spinning. Even with me grabbing my head, the pain didn't subside. Taking my head out of my heads, I looked around the room to help me remember where the hell I was. That's when I realized I had fucked up.

"What the fuck!" I yelled, making the pain in my head worse.

"What?" Atalia asked as she stirred out of her sleep.

"Bitch, is you crazy? What the fuck is you doing?"

This shit right here reminded me of why I had stopped drinking. Whenever I drank, I always ended up doing some shit I wouldn't remember the next day. I honestly hadn't even put a bottle to my mouth since my son was taken, and that was some light shit, but this bitch was stressing me out so bad that I needed something.

Atalia had the nerve to suck her teeth and roll her eyes. "Sire, please. Don't get all high and mighty now when you were definitely with the shits last night."

I don't know what came over me, but I just snapped. I reached across the bed and yanked Atalia out by her curly locs before slapping the shit out of her.

"Bitch, I wasn't with shit. You knew damn well I had some liquor in my system so you decided to take advantage of a nigga. I'll give you this one, but all I know is if my wife finds out about this shit, don't worry about Akil because I'll be snapping ya fucking neck myself," I warned her.

If that bitch ain't never took me serious before, she'd better do it now because I wasn't playing with her, and I was putting that on my mama. I hadn't even had the urge to be with another bitch since Lady came into my life but yet, here I was. I had fucked up with the worst person possible. If Lady found out about this, I had no doubts that she was going to fuck me *and* Atalia up.

I did 90 all the way home. It was still early so I was hoping that Lady would still be sleep by time I got home, so I would have time to take a shower so she wouldn't be suspicious. As luck would have it, Lady would be sitting right on the couch with Kasmira in her arms as soon as I walked through the door.

"What you doing up so early?" I asked.

Instead of answering me, Lady decided that she wanted to look at me like I was speaking a foreign language. I could already tell it was about to be some shit and I wasn't the least bit ready for it. My head was pounding and all I wanted to do was sleep off this hangover from all the liquor I had consumed the night before.

Lady got up off the couch, causing me to take a step back. Even though I didn't think she would try to swing on me with our sleeping daughter in her arms and not even knowing if she had a good reason to, I had to stay on guard when it came to her.

"You can take your disrespectful ass right on back to whatever had you so occupied that you couldn't even come home last night. I don't play those games. You got me fucked all the way up," she spoke.

Her voice was calm but I knew her, so I knew it was taking everything in her stay so calm, cool, and collected. Usually, she would not only be going off but trying to beat me upside the head. I know she wanted to blow the fuck up. Lady was the furthest thing from a hot head, but when you pushed her to the limit, you would see a completely different side of her. I learned that about Lady when Lexus thought she was going to get away with fucking with her.

Kasmira let out a little whine, so Lady readjusted her in her arms as she headed for the stairs. I stood there rubbing my head because I wasn't sure if I was beat for the shit that I knew was about to come my way. My head was pounding and I just wanted to lay down and get some sleep in peace, but I knew if it was up to Lady, nothing about this shit would be peaceful.

Fuck it, I thought as I finally made my move for the stairs. I knew eventually I was going to have to deal with it now or later, so I might as well get it over with now. When I got up the stairs, Lady was walking out of the twins' room and heading for our room, so I followed right behind her.

"Baby," I said cautiously.

Of course she ignored me and moved about the room as if I never said shit to her. I honestly didn't feel like arguing with her, so I just went ahead and headed for the bathroom. I would have to deal with her ass another time because it sure as hell wasn't about to happen now. I stopped dead in my tracks when I realized that she was taking her streets clothes off and looked as if she had been somewhere before I got home. As far as I knew, Lady was staying in the house all night with the kids, so I was confused as to where the hell she had been.

"Aye," I said as I walked out of the bathroom, just as she was finished getting undressed. Now I was really getting pissed off, because she wanted to continue to ignore me. "Stop fucking acting like you don't hear me talking to you! Where the fuck you been?" I asked as I got in her face.

"Nigga, are you fucking serious right now? You got the nerve to be questioning me about some shit when you all up in my face smelling like you just climbed from between another bitch's legs?" Lady yelled.

"I—"

"Since you really wanna fucking know, I just got home from the hospital where I had to sit with my daughter for hours because she was having a fucking asthma attack," she rolled her eyes, further making me feel like shit.

The part that was killing me was I didn't even know Kasmira had asthma, but I wasn't going to tell Lady that.

"That's my daughter, too!" was the only thing I could think of to rebuttal with.

"Nigga, please. Wanna holler that shit but couldn't even answer the fucking phone when I blew you the fuck up last night. I hope the bitch was worth it," she spat.

"Man, get the fuck outta here, wasn't nobody with no bitch! You tripping," I waved her off.

Lady didn't even bother to give me a response as she just climbed in the bed and threw the covers over her body. Lady had a lot of fight in her and I knew if she wasn't standing here trying to fight with me, she was highly pissed off. This shit had me wanting to leave and go kill Atalia for the simple fact that this bitch was causing problems in my marriage.

I don't even know why I was even dealing with her stupid ass. She definitely wasn't worth the bullshit that came along with her. The way I was feeling right now, her brother could do whatever the hell he wanted with her ass. *Fuck that bitch.*

Charmanie Saquea

Thirty-Five – Lady

"So, this bitch is a fraud?" I questioned.

I had just finished doing some digging on this Atalia bitch because something deep in my gut was telling me that she was the one Sire was with the other night. Call me crazy, but I feel like there is still some feelings on both of their parts, no matter how hard Sire tried to fight, deny, or hide it.

Call it insecure for looking into this bitch's past if you want, but I knew something wasn't adding up with this hoe and I didn't have to do the multiplication to know that. The shit I was finding out was something for the books. This bitch was really off the chain.

"This bitch is bat shit crazy, that's what she is," Lala said as we sat in her living room.

"I just wanna know why this hoe ain't locked up. They should've put this bitch under the jail," Tasha said as we continued to read on Atalia.

"Well, here it says she got off because of her insanity plea. Apparently, they did some test to find out she really is in fact crazy," Tracy informed us.

The more I dug, the more disturbed I became. It was like this hoe really needed to be locked up in somebody's penitentiary somewhere. I don't even think a mental hospital would do her ass justice.

"Oh shit, check this out, y'all. It says here that her brother is still locked up serving a life sentence," Tracy said.

"Get the fuck outta here!" I exclaimed as I rushed over to where Tracy was sitting on the floor.

Sure enough, we were looking at Virginia's inmate search and there was an Akil Patterson locked up for a lengthy time on drug charges. The fact that this girl would even lie about him being out and coming after her, was crazy. You would think that being how he was, Sire would've done his own research on the bitch instead of taking her word for it.

"Why would she lie like that though?" Lala questioned, speaking my thoughts.

"Well the bitch is certified crazy, so who the hell knows why she would do half the shit she does," Tasha said.

"You know what, I'm not dealing with this psychotic ass shit. Sire is gon' have to figure this shit out on his own. He and this bitch deserve each other. I don't need this shit."

I tried hard to bite my tongue about the situation when Sire first told me about Atalia, because I didn't want to seem like I was insecure or anything. But the fact that he actually had the nerve to try to play me like I didn't know he was up to any good is what pisses me off.

He wasn't with Toine because Lala said he was home with her that night. He wasn't with Ry because he had Ryley for the week, so he was spending time with his daughter. And Monty was still out of town with his family, so who the fuck else could he have possibly been with? That bitch, that's who.

"Lady, don't do that." Lala shook her head. "Don't make the same mistake I did by letting a random bitch come between you and the man you love. I'm not saying don't be mad at him or anything like that, but don't just give up because of this one thing. What you do is teach his ass a lesson to let him know you're not going to be having any bullshit in your marriage. Just think, this is only the beginning for you two. Your marriage is going to be tested *plenty* of times, but you can't just up and leave every time something goes wrong," she told me.

"She's right, Lady," Tracy agreed. "With Sire being who he is, your marriage is going to be put to the test a lot. You saw that before you two even got married."

I just sat there and twiddled my thumbs as I thought about what Lala and Tracy were telling me. My relationship with Sire has definitely gone through the ringer since we've been together. This was the same man that threw me out of his house and I almost died behind, but yet, I still found it in my heart to forgive and love him after that.

Cheating, though? That was something I wasn't sure I could handle. It wasn't like it was just some random bitch, not that that would make the situation any better. But he actually had a connection to this woman. This was his first love, the first woman that ever held his heart. I can't compete with that and I shouldn't have to.

-$-

"Shit," I cursed as I dropped one of the bags I was carrying.

I hiked one of the other bags up on my shoulder before bending down to pick it up. I sighed as I opened the front door but before I could even step out, I was greeted by none other than Kasire. This was the exact thing I was trying to avoid. He eyed the bags I was carrying before his eyes landed on me. I had to prepare myself for the fight that I knew was about to go down.

"Where we going?" he asked as he stood in the doorway.

"We're not going anywhere; I'm leaving for a while," I told him.

The moment I said that, I saw something pass in his eyes and I knew then that the crazy part of him had officially come out. *Here we go.*

"What the fuck you mean you leaving for a while? Aye, don't even answer that stupid shit. Just know you got me fucked up and you better take them bags right back upstairs," he said, as he walked up on me and slightly pushed me back.

"Alright, Kasire. I already done told you about putting your fucking hands on me," I warned him.

"I ain't put my hands on you yet, but I will if you keep this shit up. What the fuck is even wrong with you? You been on some other shit lately and you better get it together," he had the nerve to say.

The audacity of this nigga, I thought to myself as I dropped my bags. He was talking to me as if *I* was the one who had fucked up. What he wasn't about to do was spin this shit around on me, with his crazy ass.

"I been on some other shit? Nigga, you fucked a whole other bitch then had the nerve to walk through my front door like shit was cool. I don't know what the fuck you are used to doing with the bitches before me, but I'm not letting that shit fly. Fuck you and her, now, goodbye," I spat as I picked my bags back up.

"That's what the fuck this shit is about? Okay, fuck it. Yea, I fucked the bitch, but I didn't have any intentions on doing so, and I put that on my mama. I got too fucking drunk and that bitch took advantage of that shit. I don't want that hoe!" he yelled.

I looked at him like he was stupid because not a damn word that was coming out of his mouth was making me feel any better.

"You think I give a fuck?" I yelled back. "Nigga, you shouldn't have even been with that bitch in the first place. What type of hold that bitch got on you where you can't see that she ain't shit? Since that's how we doing shit, let me go out and fuck the next nigga to—"

WHAP!

Silly of me to think I could say something crazy like that and Sire not react. Before I could even finish saying what I had to say, this nigga had slapped the shit out of me and had me in the air by my fucking neck. Sire was way taller than me so my feet were literally dangling in the air.

"Bitch, you got me fucked up. Don't ever let me hear no shit like that come out your fucking mouth. Do you not know that I will kill you and that nigga?"

I don't know what the fuck had happened, but Sire wasn't sounding like himself and he had this crazed look in his eyes. I feared that I was going to lose my life from the death grip he had on my throat, as I tried to claw at his hands to get him to let me go.

Right when I thought I was going to pass out, he put me back on the ground and let my throat go. I felt light headed as hell, as I tried to get all the oxygen to flow by through my body. I looked at Sire like he had completely lost his fucking mind. He had the nerve to shrug his shoulders like it wasn't shit, and walked away.

Something in me snapped and I picked up the lamp off the table that was by the front door, and lunged it at his ass. It hit him right in the back of his big, bald ass head. His hand went up to the spot where the lamp hit him and before he could even turn around, I was charging at him.

"You crazy—"

"Ahhh!" I yelled as I jumped on him and started hitting him wherever my punches could land. When I figured that wasn't doing shit for me, I bit his ass right in his chest. I sank my teeth in him deep enough to penetrate his skin, and I didn't give a fuck.

I wasn't about to just stay here and let this nigga think it was okay to put his hands on me.

"Fuuuck!" he yelled out in agony as I finally took my teeth out of him.

I knew he wasn't going to let me get away with that, so I tried to run away, but he grabbed me back by my ponytail.

"Have you lost yo' fucking mind?" his voice boomed.

"Let me go!" I said as I jabbed him right in his face.

I paused with my mouth open when I saw that I had hit him in his nose. He put his hand up to his nose and that's when I saw the blood. A part of me wanted to care and feel bad for hitting him, but the other part of me was yelling for me to get the fuck out of there before I died, so that was the part I listened to.

Sire had this deadly look in his eyes as I snatched my car keys off the floor and made a dash for the door. I could hear his heavy footsteps behind me as I ran out of the house and to my car that I was happy that I left unlocked.

"Lady!" he yelled.

I ignored him and got into my car, immediately locking the door so he couldn't get in. He banged on the car window, smearing his blood on it, to get me to open the door. But I wasn't crazy. I literally saw my life flash before my eyes when I hit Sire, and I wasn't ready to die. I backed out of the driveway as Sire continued to bang on the window before I sped off.

I don't know what the fuck was wrong with us, but I knew we needed to get far away from each other as possible. The shit we were doing right now wasn't even cool, and I was happy that my kids weren't there to witness that. I don't know where we were going to go from here, but we needed some time apart so we could both calm down.

Charmanie Saquea

Thirty-Six – Lala

"Hello, officers, may I help you?" Terrance, Tracy's husband asked two men that walked into the building.

I was sitting behind my desk, minding my own business, but hearing that caused my attention to go somewhere else. The men didn't have uniforms on so I wasn't sure how Terrance knew they were the police.

"Do you have an Alani Martin working here?" one of the officers asked, as they flashed their badge.

Now I was sitting there confused because I had no idea why the police would be looking for me. I knew I hadn't done anything illegal so this had to be some type of mistake.

"May I ask what you want with her?" Terrance asked.

"What's wrong?" Tracy asked as she stopped in front of my desk.

"Apparently, they're here for me," I said with my eyes still trained on them.

"What? For what?" Tracy asked.

"I have no idea," I answered.

I was so busy talking with Tracy that I missed what the reason was for. When I looked up, they were walking in my direction. Tracy just stood there like she wasn't moving until she got to the bottom of things.

"Ms. Martin? I'm Detective Hans, and this is my partner, Detective Mills. Do you mind if we ask you a few questions about your boyfriend?" he asked, as he pulled out a small notebook from his pocket.

"What type of questions?" Tracy asked before I could say anything.

"I'm sorry, and you are?" Detective Mills asked like he had an attitude or something.

"I'm her lawyer, and I'm making sure this line of questioning goes smoothly," Tracy said with a smirk. "You know, it is her right to have her lawyer present when she's being questioned."

I fought hard to hide the smile that was threatening to escape my lips because the look on their faces was truly one for the books. I don't know what they expected, though. I did work at a law firm so they should've been prepared for something like this.

"Very well then," Detective Hans cleared his throat. "When was the last time you heard from your boyfriend, Darius Meeks?"

he asked.

Darius? I thought to myself. I just knew they were coming here to question me about some shit that had to do with Toine. It wouldn't have been the first time I had been through this. Years ago when Toine and I were together and still young, I was questioned about his street business, but I couldn't give them anything because Toine never told me shit. He still doesn't to this day.

To my surprise, they were actually here to talk about Darius's ass. I almost had to correct them to let them know he wasn't my boyfriend, but I didn't want to give them any reason to think I had something to do with his case.

"Umm, it's been a few days. Maybe a week now," I said.

"A few days or a week?" Detective Mills asked.

"Well, a few days can be a week so we'll go with a week," I replied smartly.

"You didn't find that quite odd? To go that long without talking to your boyfriend?"

"No. Darius was known to go short periods of time without keeping in contact with me. He claimed he was always working so I just waited for him to pop back up when he was ready," I answered honestly.

I didn't have anything to hide when it came to Darius but at the same time, I wasn't going to give them anything where it would lead them to Toine. Darius was responsible for his own death, so they might as well rule it a suicide.

"Did you know that he was married?"

"Married?" I asked truly shocked.

"Yes, his wife is the one who initially reported him missing," Detective Hans informed me.

Now, I could've sat up here and been upset, but I felt like I had no reason to be. Even though Darius had deceived me the whole relationship, I was deceiving him as well. It was wrong for me to lead that man on when I knew damn well that my heart still belonged to Toine. That was one of the main reasons I couldn't accept his proposal. Even though that shit turned out to be fake, seeing how his ass was already married.

"Are you sure this wasn't a lover's quarrel? You didn't get jealous or angry when you found out about his wife then had somebody take him out?" Detective Mills questioned or more so accused, as he looked at me with an evil look.

"I—"

"Okay, so this is where I end this. My client isn't a suspect, right? So therefore, please find the nearest exit," Tracy stepped in before I could light into his ass.

I wasn't feeling what his pale faced ass was trying to insinuate. What the fuck I look like getting his ass killed over some shit like that? Hell, I know how crazy my kids' father is and I didn't even want him to find out about the incident between Darius and I because I knew without a doubt that Toine would kill him.

"Alani, don't worry about them. I know you're innocent, so I'll make sure they never bother you again," Tracy assured me before she walked away.

After that, my whole mood was shot. I just wanted to go home and clear my mind and free it up of all the bullshit. Darius was no longer a factor in my life, so I refused to let this incident get the best of me.

Charmanie Saquea

Thirty-Seven – Sire

"Why are you moping around my house?" my mom asked, as she burst into the room I was lying down in.

"Damn, Ma, I can't just come chill at yo' crib for a while?" I asked.

"Hell no! Go chill at home...with your wife." She rolled her eyes as she opened the blinds in my room.

It had been almost two weeks since Lady left me and I was sick. Literally. It was as if I couldn't function and didn't want to do shit without her, but just lie in the bed. If I didn't know any better, I would say that a nigga was slightly depressed.

"That house is not a home when she's not there," I sighed. "Besides, ain't you going to get the kids?" I asked.

Even though I haven't seen Lady in two weeks, I saw the kids every day. My mom went to go get them from the house Lady was staying at, and brought them to see me. That was another thing that had me in my feelings. Why the hell did Lady have a secret house that I didn't know about? Why did she need another house? It was shit like that that I didn't like.

"Okay, first of all, stay out my Luther Vandross CDs but nope.

I'm tired of playing the middle man. If you want to see your kids, then I suggest you go make up with their mama because I'm staying out of the shit," she informed me.

"Ma," I sighed as I ran my hands down my face. "I can't, you know she ain't messing with me right now. She thinks I wanna kill her."

"Do you still have feelings for her?"

I looked at my mama like she had just said the wrong thing. That was like asking me did I need oxygen to breathe or something.

"Of course I have feelings for her mom, she's my wife. I—"

"I'm not talking 'bout Lady. I have no doubt that you have feelings for, or love her. I'm talking about that fast tail little girl I told you to leave alone years ago, but you chose not to listen to me until it was too late," she said, as she folded her arms over her chest.

I had to sit up on my elbows and give my mom a funny look. The shit that just flew out of her mouth came so out of left field that I don't even know if I wanted to respond to that. I was tired of people thinking that I actually gave a fuck about Atalia when that was the furthest thing from the truth.

"Fuck no!" I blurted out, forgetting who I was talking to. "Excuse my language, Ma, but this ain't ten years ago and I'm not that dumb teenage nigga no more," I let her know.

What I needed for people to realize is that Atalia and Lady were at two different points in my life. What I had with Atalia was some puppy love, teenage, high school shit. Of course, back then I thought the shit was going to last going to last forever, but obviously it didn't.

With Lady, this is the real deal. I've never loved someone the way I love her little ass; not even Atalia. We've been through some shit that I just know we wouldn't be able to make it through, but we stuck together through it all…until now. I guess Lady finally had enough of my shit.

"Oh really?" my mom asked. "If that's the case, then why was it so easy for this heffa to weasel her way back in and fuck up your marriage? If you're not dumb, why the hell would you get involved with her stupid ass again knowing what she did to you the first time? I hope your marriage was worth it, Kasire. I really do."

"Ma, I—"

"Shut the hell up talking to me and go see about your wife and kids. You better hope and pray that Lady's strong willed ass forgives you and takes you back. Don't come crying to me if she doesn't, you brought this on yourself," my mom fussed, as she placed a small piece of paper on my bed.

As ruthless as I was in the streets, I knew better than to say anything back to my mom when she was going off on me. Especially when it had anything to do with her precious little Lady. Ever since I brought her home that day, she was quick to throw me to the curb over her.

I watched her as she left the room, still fussing of course, before I picked up the paper. On it, she had written down an address that wasn't too far from here. I'm guessing it's where Lady had been staying and she really wanted me to take my ass over there.

-$-

I stood with my hands stuffed in my pockets as I waited for Lady to come to the door. Knowing that this would literally be the first time that I would be laying eyes on Lady since that crazy day at the house, had me anxious as hell. Just thinking about that day, a small smile came across my face. I still couldn't believe Lady really hit me in my shit like that. Her little ass really hit hard as fuck.

"I'mma call you back," she said as she opened the door, snapping me out of my thoughts.

348

For a while, neither one of us said anything. We just stood there staring at each other. Tired of playing this little game with her, I walked closer to her, but she flinched and jumped back like I was going to hit her or something. No lie, that shit hurt like hell.

"Don't do that, you ain't gotta be scared of me," I told her.

"What do you want, Kasire?" she asked.

I knew anytime she called me by my full name instead of calling me Sire, I was in some serious shit. I could just look at her and see the hurt in her eyes and I hated this shit. It was never in my intentions to hurt Lady. If I could go back and change this shit, I swear to God I would.

"You, I miss you. I want you. I want you and my kids to come home. I want you to forgive me. I want us to move past this shit and go back to the way things were before this shit even happened," I told her.

Lady folded her arms over her chest, tilted her head to the side and looked at me like I had shit on my face. I knew then she wasn't about to give in so easily—she never did. That was the shit I loved but hated about her at the same time; she could be too damn stubborn.

Lady went to open her mouth to say something but before she

could get it out, one of the kids' cries cut her off. She immediately turned around and took off running in the house, so I followed her in, shutting the door behind me. I was about to run after her, but a piece of paper laying on her coffee table caught my attention.

I picked it up and looked over it in shock. The more I read, the more heated I got. Apparently, Lady had printed some shit off about Atalia but that wasn't why I was mad.

"There's Daddy," Lady said as she walked back in the room.

I looked up from the papers at her as she held KJ in her arms, then back to the papers.

"This shit serious?" I asked.

"Yea," Lady somberly answered.

"That bitch killed my son," I stated in disbelief as I read the papers.

According to what I had just read, Atalia had drowned her three-year-old son in the tub four years ago and if the numbers added up, that child would've been mine. A son I had no idea she was even pregnant with at the time. What was even more crazier to me was the fact that they let this bitch get off because they claimed she was crazy.

"That's not all, Sire. She's been playing you this whole time.

350

Check a few more pages back," Lady said.

I looked through the pages until I found a paper with Akil's inmate photo and information on it. According to his earliest release date, this nigga wasn't getting out for another 15 years. I ran my hand down my beard and let out a laugh. Once again, I had let this bitch play me.

I looked up at Lady and realized besides my mom, she really is the only female that ever came into my life and kept it solid with me. To know that I really risked that over a bitch that not only crossed me once but twice, meant I really didn't deserve her.

I dropped the papers on the floor and made a dash for the door with nothing on my mind but murder.

"Kasire!" Lady yelled after me.

I couldn't even stop to see what she wanted. I had to make this shit right and there was only one way I could do that: get rid of Atalia's no good ass once and for all, like I should've done years ago.

Charmanie Saquea

Thirty-Eight – Toine

"Welcome to Las Vegas!" Lala yelled. "Yassss!"

On some spur of the moment shit, Lala got the idea to come to Vegas with all four of our kids. There was no way I could tell her no, so I instantly started looking for flights on the first thing smoking.

"You a little hype, ain't you?" I laughed, as we walked down the strip.

"Yes, I've never been here before," she smiled as she looked around.

"What made you wanna come here all of a sudden?" I asked as I opened the juice Antoinette was reaching for.

Lala stopped pushing the stroller and looked at me with a smile that was a mile long. "To be honest, I wanted to get married…today," she said. "That's only if you still want me to be your wife," she quickly added.

I stopped to look at her to see if she was serious. She hadn't put her ring back on or even mentioned the engagement since we had been working things out, so I can't lie, I was a little taken back that she wanted to get married right now.

"You don't want to get married anymore?" she asked with a sad look on her face.

"What? Nah, hell nah! That's not the case, La. I'm just trying to make sure that this is what you really want. I'm just a little caught off guard because I thought you was feeling like…you know," I told her.

"Toine, I just, I don't know. You know when you have been together for years, your relationship takes a lot of hits. We've been through so much since we've been little, but through it all my love for you has never changed. You were there for me at one of the worst times of my life. Any other nigga would've just pulled the plug on me and let me die, but you didn't. You were there with me every step of the way. I understand that nobody is perfect and I don't want perfect, I want you," she poured out her heart right there on the strip.

I always knew Lala had love for me, but lately she had me questioning and wondering if she was still in love with me. I had seen couples who went from loving each other unconditionally to hating each other's guts, and I didn't want that for us.

"So kids, how do you feel about me and your mom getting married?" I asked.

Heaven was looking at a lengthy time behind bars, so I filed for

354

custody of both of my kids. They deserved a better life than what they trifling ass mama ass mama had been giving them for the past two years. Since being with me, they were back to their normal happy selves and even had been calling Lala mom lately.

I didn't have any qualms about that because she had been in their lives since they were born and treated them like they were hers. The way I see it, she treated them better than their mama did.

Lala let out a giggle as the kids whispered amongst themselves like they really had to have a discussion about it. When they were done, AJ cleared his throat.

"We the people have talked amongst ourselves, and we would like to know...what took you so long? Gosh," AJ said.

"No you didn't, little boy!" Lala laughed.

"No, for real though, Dad. We think that you two should go ahead and do it. We've only been waiting for forever."

"You better get your son before I hurt him," Lala told me.

"That's all you," I told her.

I couldn't do anything but laugh because my kids had some wild personalities. Sometimes they acted like their moms, sometimes they acted like me, and half the time I don't know who the hell they acted like.

-$-

"I can't believe we did it!" Lala gushed.

I was now officially a married man. I was the second member of the goon squad to be tied down and I couldn't lie, the shit felt good as hell.

"Why not? I told you I was going to make an honest woman out of you, girl."

"That you did baby, that you did," she smiled, before kissing my lips.

"Ewe."

"Nasty!"

"We really don't wanna see that," was all we heard from behind us from our big head ass kids.

I just shook my head as I reached into my pocket to answer my ringing phone.

"It's Sire," I told Lala before answering. "What's up, nigga?"

"Where the fuck you at, nigga?"

"You wouldn't even believe me if I told you," I said.

"Try me."

"I'm in Vegas, and before you even ask, I just got married," I told him proudly.

The line went quiet before Sire's voice boomed in my ear. "Get the fuck outta here! Lala finally locked yo' baby making ass down?" he yelled.

I should've known his stupid ass was going to be the one who was going to talk shit. He was the only one who would never let me forget the fact that I had a whole lot of kids. No matter how many jokes his ass had, he loved his nieces and nephews to death.

"Yea, she did. I was about to give up on her ass and find somebody else," I said, talking shit.

Lala rolled her eyes at me and waved me off, letting what I said go in one ear and out the other.

"Damn, well, two of us down, two more to go. I'm happy for you, bro. I guess I'll save the bullshit and let you enjoy your honeymoon," Sire said.

Just by the change of tone of his voice, I could tell that something was wrong with him. I knew he was going through it with Lady and that had him sick, but it sounded like it was something else going on.

"What's wrong?"

"Nah, it's cool, Toine. I just got hit with some crazy shit, but I'm not going to even bother you with it right now," he said.

"Aye, don't make any moves until I get back," I told him.

"I got you," he said before hanging up.

"What happened, now?" Lala asked.

"I don't know; he wouldn't tell me," I shrugged.

I don't know what the hell is going on, but I was hoping everything was alright with Sire. It seemed as if every time things were going good for all of us, we always got hit with some shit out of nowhere. It never failed.

Thirty-Nine – Ry

"What else I need?" I asked Candace as she pushed the cart down the aisle.

Our relationship had been going way better than I thought it would. It was way less awkward than I thought it would be, and it was nothing but good vibes between us. Not to mention that my mama loved her, which was a big plus for the both of us.

Tonight, I was hosting date night at my house and since I had nothing at my house to eat according to her, we had to come to get everything we needed so she could cook us dinner.

"You need a lot, Ry. You literally have nothing at your house to eat. I don't see how you haven't died from starvation yet," she shook her head.

I couldn't argue with her on that one because she wasn't lying. I wasn't the grocery shopping type of nigga and I haven't had a woman in my house to do the grocery shopping in years, so I always ate at my mama's house. Even when Ryley comes over my house for the weekends, we ate at my mama's house or stocked up on junk food against Tasha's wishes.

"See, that's why I need you around to make sure I eat," I smiled.

"Mm hmm, now grab two boxes of spaghetti noodles," she said.

"Damn that's cold." I laughed at how she had just brushed me off. "I surely hope you know what you doing," I told her.

"What, you don't have faith in my cooking?" she asked with a raised eyebrow.

"I'm just saying, females always brag about how much they can cook until you actually get them in the kitchen and they damn near burn the house down."

"Interesting," she said. "I really don't know what type of water boiling, ramen noodles cooking females you been dealing with in the past, but that ain't never been my story. Every female in my family started off in the kitchen, young. My grandma didn't play that stuff. I was in the kitchen cooking before I was 10 years old. I can show you better than I can tell you," Candace said, getting me all the way together.

"Damn. Alright, Candy Girl, I hear you."

"You better or your ass won't be eating shit." She playfully rolled her eyes.

"You—"

"Damn, what's up Candace. Long time no see. I didn't even know you was back in town," I heard from behind me, cutting me off from what I was about to say.

"Hey, J," Candace smiled, even though I could tell it was forced.

I turned to see who she was talking to. The nigga she was speaking to, smile dropped from his face when I turned around, and was replaced with a mug. I instantly got the motion that he knew her ex nigga. I knew he didn't know me personally to have any beef with me, so that was the only reason for his sudden mood change.

"Damn, that's how you doing it now? What type of shit is this?" he spat in fury.

"Don't do that, J, please don't," Candace said as she grabbed my hand. "Come on, Ry." She tried to walk away.

I was actually going to be nice this time because I know this was a fucked up situation for her, and I didn't want to make it any more awkward for her than it already was. So instead of getting ignorant with the nigga, I did as she said and walked away, sparing him.

"I never thought I would see the day where you would be fucking the nigga that killed Fiq! That's some hoe ass shit, Candace. I knew you wasn't shit, bitch!" he yelled after her.

That's when I said to hell with this playing nice shit. Niggas just didn't know when to leave well enough alone.

"Ryan, no!" Candace yelled, but it was too late.

I grabbed one of the cans off the shelf and bust his stupid ass in the face with it, breaking his nose instantly. I then proceeded to pull my gun out from my waistline, shoving it in his mouth while knocking his front teeth out.

"What the fuck you just say, bitch? Nah, don't get quiet on me now. You just had all that mouth a few seconds ago! If you ever, and I do mean ever disrespect my girl again, I will blow yo' fucking tongue out the back of yo' fucking head. You better spread the message that Candace is Ry's girl now and he ain't having that shit, so muthafuckas better think twice the next time they wanna approach her on some fuck shit," I spat, as I shoved the gun further in his mouth, making him gag on it before I took it out.

I wiped the blood and spit off on his shirt before standing up and stuffing it back in my waistline. To my surprise, Candace didn't even look scared or surprised by what had just happened. I looked deep in her eyes and saw that she was calm.

"Maybe we should get out of here. I'm pretty sure one of these white people done called the police by now. Fucking around with you, we gotta eat pizza tonight," she said.

I just laughed because after what the fuck just happened, the only thing she was mad about was the fact that she had to eat pizza. *Lord, where did this woman come from?*

-$-

"So, nigga, when you gonna stop playing and marry Cola?" I asked Monty as we sat in my Ry Cave, smoking.

I guess love had truly been in the air, because these niggas were around here getting married like it was going out of style. No lie though, I was happy as hell for Toine and Sire, especially Toine. That nigga had been chasing after Lala since before his balls had even dropped, and they finally were one.

Hearing me ask him that caused Monty to choke on the blunt he was smoking. Everyone started laughing because he was so fucking dramatic.

"Nigga, what? Me? Married? Hell nah!" he waved the idea off.

"What's that supposed to mean? If Sire can get married, anybody can get married," Toine said.

"Yea, and you see his stupid ass was barely married a month

363

and already fucked that shit up," Monty laughed. "No thank you."

I damn near fell off the couch in laughter at the death stare that Sire was giving Monty. The separation between he and Lady was a very touchy subject for him. They had been trying to work on it but of course, Lady wouldn't be her if she didn't make it hard on his ass. She was literally making this nigga kiss her ass to make it up to her for him fucking Atalia's dog ass, and I can't really say I blame her.

"Nigga, fuck you!" Sire spat.

"Oh shit! He said that from the bottom of his heart." I laughed even harder.

"Man, all y'all niggas can eat a dick," Sire said. "Here go my wife right here," he said as he answered his ringing phone.

"They crazy as hell." Toine shook his head.

I sat up in my seat when I noticed the look on Sire's face. I knew my brother well enough to know when he was ready to kill, and right now he had the look of murder on his face.

"What's wrong, Si?" I questioned, getting everybody else's attention.

Instead of answering, Sire put his hand up to his mouth to signal for us to be quiet as he put his phone on speaker. We heard a commotion on Lady's end before what sounded like a gun cocking.

"It was never supposed to be you! He was supposed to love me!"

Atalia? I thought to myself.

"Bitch, I know you got a millisecond to get that fucking gun away from my daughter. Just because you killed your child don't mean I'm gonna let you even think you can kill either of mines," we heard Lady say.

When Sire heard that, he instantly jumped out of his seat and headed for the stairs with all of us right on his heels. This was starting to turn into some fatal attraction type shit. Sire said he went back to the hotel Atalia was staying at, to kill her ass, but she had checked out. Yet, here she was trying to kill Lady and his kids.

"This bitch got me fucked up!" Sire yelled.

"I'll drive!" I yelled with my keys already in my hand.

Times like this, I was happy that Sire only stayed two blocks away because this was an emergency situation. We didn't have time to be driving all over Richmond to get to wherever the fuck we needed to be. My sister, niece, and nephews' lives were in danger.

In literally two minutes tops, we made it to Sire's house. All four of us jumped out of the car and followed behind Sire, as he led the way to into his house, damn near kicking the door in with his gun already drawn.

When we got in, Lady was standing in the middle of the floor with a crying Kasmira in her arms, with not a KJ or Kasim in sight. I kept my gun trained on Atalia while my brother walked right in front of Lady as if Atalia didn't even have a gun trained on her.

"You good?" he asked her.

"Yea, this crazy bitch been following us and shit. I'm good, but she got my baby shook up," Lady spat.

I could tell that she was more pissed off about the fact that Atalia was pulling this shit while her kids were here than anything else. Anyone who knew Lady knew that her world revolved around her kids.

"Where the boys?" he asked.

"Playing in the game room," she answered.

"Really, Kasire!" Atalia yelled. "You're going to ignore me like I'm not even standing here? I will kill you and this bitch!"

"Toine, can you get my kids, please?" Sire asked, as he kissed his daughter and told her everything was going to be okay.

Without hesitation, Toine took Kasmira from Lady's arm and made his way to the game room where the boys were. Sire made a move to turn around and continued to stand in front of Lady, protecting her like a real man would.

"Bitch, yo' looney ass wanted my attention and now you got it. What? What the fuck could you possibly want?" he asked.

"What do I want? Sire, don't play with me, okay? You know what I want! I want you to love me! You never loved me!" Atalia irately yelled.

"You're right," he shrugged. "I could never love a bitch who would think it was okay to drown her own son. Who does that type of shit."

The fuck? I was so lost in this whole thing. I didn't know what son or drowning Sire was talking about. He failed to mention that little part to me.

A crazy looking smile came over Atalia's face. "He...he was so cute, Sire. He looked just like you. We can make another one. We can make another one and be a family like we're supposed to be. That's why I came back. To be a family."

"This bitch is crazy," Lady said.

"Shut the fuck up, bitch!" Atalia yelled as she pointed her gun at Lady, which meant she was pointing it at Sire. "I'm not crazy!"

"Yo, what part of I don't want you do you not understand? You were a fucking mistake! A mistake that never should've happened. I regret ever sticking my dick in you. You—"

POW!

Time stood still as I watched my brother's body hit the ground. I heard Lady scream his name as she fell to her knees and cradled his body in her arms, but I still couldn't move. I heard another gunshot go off but this time, Atalia's body dropped to the ground with half of her head missing.

I turned towards Monty to see the smoke coming from his gun. Slowly, I turned back to my brother and Lady, but I still couldn't move.

"Sire, baby, please! Don't do this to me! The kids need you! I need you!" Lady yelled as the tears fell from her eyes.

"Si...Sire." Suddenly it felt as if my throat was dry.

"NOOOOOO!" Lady let out a wail I had never heard before, as Monty held her in his arms.

I fell back into the back of the couch as Toine rushed back into the room with a somber look on his face. We exchanged looks and it was then that we knew our lives would be changed forever. After everything we had been through, all the dirt we had done together, all the good times and the bad times, it was coming to an end like this.

Damn.

Charmanie Saquea

Epilogue – Lady

Six Months Later…

"Lady you…I know you are not?" Cola fussed at me.

I sniffled as to hide the fact that I was once again crying. It had been very hard for me to control my emotions today, and I hated it. The woman who took pride in usually being able to have a handle on her emotions, had been all over the place for the past few months.

"You know he wouldn't want you to be in here crying," Cola told me as she wiped my tears.

"I know, Co," I sighed. "I just can't help it."

"Ohh, somebody's a little excited to hear your voice. Let that cheer you up," she smiled, as she placed my hand on her stomach.

I let out a giggle as I felt the kicks of her very active son. Monty had finally succeeded in knocking Cola up, despite her fears, and even went as far as to propose to her with all that shit he was talking. Now, we were anxiously awaiting the arrival of our new prince to the family, and the next wedding.

"I know your ass ain't in here crying again!" Lala yelled.

"She was, but we have everything taken care of. Ain't that

371

right?" Cola winked at me.

"Okay, good. Now let's go."

Putting a smile on my face, I followed Cola and Lala out of the bathroom before they ended up having to drag me out of it. I took a deep breath to get myself together as they led me back into the ballroom.

"Okay everyone, it's time for the groom and bride's first dance," the DJ announced.

Before I could even turn to look for him, I felt a strong pair of arms wrap around me, and that beard I loved so much tickle my neck.

"I thought you ran off on me," he said, as he led me to the middle of the floor, still wrapped in his arms.

"Never," I smiled.

"Yo' ass was probably in there crying...again," he smiled.

I couldn't do anything but laugh from embarrassment. I was so overcome with emotion because I was actually having the wedding that I never thought I would have, especially after that looney tunes ass bitch, Atalia, forced her way into my house six months ago.

When Sire got shot in his chest, I thought I had lost him for good that time, but God had different plans for us. The ambulance came and was able to revive him. My baby fought hard to come back to me and his kids. After he woke up, the first thing he said was my ass needed to start back planning that wedding I wanted to have.

I wasted no time getting back to it. So, here I was, today, having my first dance with my husband, to "You" by Jesse Powell. After everything we had been through since the first day we met, we were finally able to put all the shit behind us and live happily and peacefully. Just us and our three kids.

"So, about that other baby," Sire said.

"What baby?" I asked, playing dumb.

"You remember our deal. Don't play. You got your wedding, so now I want my baby," he said.

I laughed and laid my head onto his chest because there was something that I had been wanting to tell him for the past week, but I hadn't found the right time. Now that he was bringing it up, I guess now was the perfect time.

"Well, daddy, I guess you'll be getting it sooner than you think," I said, as I rubbed my stomach.

Sire stepped back and looked at me with the biggest smile I had ever seen on his face.

"Oh shit, that boy strikes again," he said, like he was so geeked.

I playfully rolled my eyes because I didn't know how to feel about this. All of Sire's kids had attitudes like him, and that wasn't a good thing. I at least wanted one child to come out with my personality.

"Damn, what if we have another set of twins?" he asked.

"Oh, hell no! You going too far now," I shook my head.

"I'm just saying. You never know," he shrugged.

"God would never be that cruel to me," I said.

"Whatever, dude."

I laughed before kissing his lips.

"I love you, Mr. Lewis."

"I love you more, Mrs. Lewis."

THE END

Contact Charmanie Saquea

Facebook: Charmanie Saquea

Twitter: xoCharm_

Instagram: iam.saquea

Readers Group: Charmanie's Queendom

Text **CHARM** to **42828** to stay up to date on future releases

Looking for a publishing home?

Royalty Publishing House, Where the Royals reside, is accepting submissions for writers in the urban fiction genre. If you're interested, submit the first 3-4 chapters with your synopsis to submissions@royaltypublishinghouse.com. Check out our website for more information: www.royaltypublishinghouse.com.

Be sure to LIKE our Royalty Publishing House

page on Facebook

COMING NEXT!

Did you grab our last #Royal release?

Do You Like CELEBRITY GOSSIP? Check Out QUEEN DYNASTY!

Like Our Page HERE! Visit Our Site:

www.thequeendynasty.com

HAVE YOU CLICKED ON THESE

RELEASES?

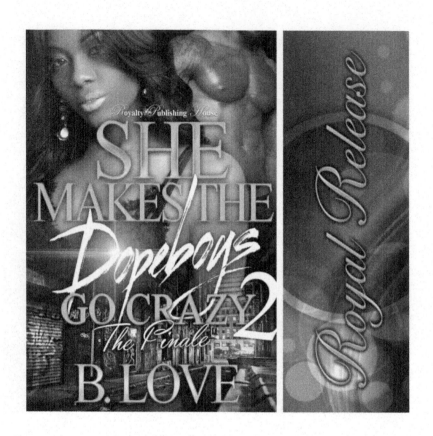

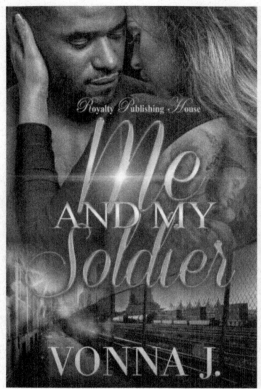

CPSIA information can be obtained
at www.ICGtesting.com
Printed in the USA
LVOW13s1606130117

520897LV00010B/639/P